ROXXY

****

A.C. BELLARD

First Printing: 2016

ISBN- 978-1-7324049-0-8

Published by Ricky Gaines

Cover Design: F. Ruiz

Senior Editor: A. Parra

Assistant Editor: Ricky Gaines

Capital Gaines LLC
4023 Kennett Pike #2082
Wilmington DE 19807
Email: cg@capitalgaines.com
Website: www.capgainesllc.com
Phone: 302-433-6777

Acknowledgements

Spanish language contributors:
Candelario, "Pantera" and R. Ventura, "Toons".

Roxxy is dedicated to Alex's daughter, Tabora K. Briggs, granddaughter, Natale, and grandson, Kimani Freeman,

Love, Peace, & Prosperity,
Alex
aka AC Bellard

Dedication

This novel is dedicated to big dreamers, to real hustlers, and to the usefulness of transferable skills...

To our Capital Gaines LLC team - Thank you for having the courage, faith, and confidence to stick with me on this legitimate, creative mission.

To the author - A.C. Bellard,
Congratulations. You've done it again Sir. The story is superb, and it has been a pleasure to publish.

Cheers to longevity, healthy living, and even bigger dreams.
To our friends, family, supporters, and readers from every culture - all over the world, THANK YOU, THANK YOU, THANK YOU.

Enjoy the novel, and please, spread the word.

Ricky Gaines / Slick-G / Publisher

ROXXY

****

A.C. BELLARD

CHAPTER ONE

Stinger

HO MONEY IS NOT necessarily slow money and sometimes I do get mine in chunks. My name is Roxanne Blackwell. My tricks call me Candy Cane, 'cause I'm a redheaded chick, five ten, all legs with plenty of curves in all the right places. I got into the 'hook an' trick' game early. Age fourteen. A runaway from a boarding school. It ain't no new story, ha. Actually, I'm tired of tellin' it, so I'll save the sordid details for some other time. But on second thought, I'll at least say this...

I ran into a smooth talking, hustler-pimp, a whatever, named Slick. You know the type. Real sharply dressed, clean cut with a goatee and rockin' the latest designer gear. He was athletically built, he always smelt great, and reminded me of smooth money. When he wasn't runnin' at the mouth, he spent the majority of his time detailing his car or just poppin' his collar in any body's mirror, even more than me. I met him right after this irate trucker dumped my ass along a stretch of interstate desert up near Barstow, California.

Slick's cocaine-white S-500 Mercedes Benz sittin' on 22'chrome rims appeared like a mirage and swept me off my feet like Don Juan. You know, the real flamboyant type, extremely confident in his game. He wasn't anything like these new booties who claim they're pimps but in actuality they be pimpin' their girlfriends. Oh' hell nah, I'm not one to be easily persuaded or brainwashed for that matter.

That so-called 'sweet-talk', "I'm the one that loves you, 'cause nobody else cares, I got you, …yada, yada, yada." But I do like a little intrigue and adventure. Besides, a man can put me under his spell gently, but don't come at me soft then hard, 'cause I ain't buying that passive aggressive shit. If you abuse me once, well, I ain't gonna give you a second chance. I'll ditch you like a "Kardashian", and believe me I'm gonna get mine's first.

Well, I never had to be concerned with too much runnin'. I played along with Mista Slick's idea of romance and swoon. He carted me off to Las Vegas. Of course he thought he was nickel-slick and turned me over to a couple of other chicks he had under his wing. They were setting up Johns and rolling them. Not every John, only when the occasion called for it. Eventually, the 'Big Brother' cameras got 'em on tape and exposed their dumb asses. Luckily for me, I was walking my beat when the shit hit the fan. So I scurried my ass away and hitched a diesel to Silicon Valley, the electronics capitol. I must of read about it somewhere. It was there that I allowed myself to be swept up, yet once again by another smooth ass hustler-pimp at the Greyhound depot in downtown San Jose, CA.

* * *

It was a typical cool Thursday evening in the South Bay. By midnight I had finished my rounds of the usual clientele, a sleazy corporate lawyer and a balding three hundred pound mortician. When I turned the key and cracked the door to my 11th floor condo at Terra Cotta Heights, breezy jazz licks from a Paul Hardcastle CD spilled into the dimly lit hallway. Instantly, I knew I had uninvited guests.

Moe Betta Butts, the guy who helped me off the streets and into his penthouse a couple years back, was working my private bar. He was pouring himself a stiff shot of Chivas. Five-six, blue-black, with bulbous eyes, the two-bit gambler had some game, but I allowed him to think he was shrewder then me. Moe walked with a gimp. He says he was born that way but I suspect that somebody had once busted him in a kneecap over a bet that was never paid.

Sprawled on my white lambskin couch was a big buffed Shotgun Bob Johnson and his scrawny-ass willowy lookin' girlfriend, Wilma Sarpy. She was clinging to Bob like spaghetti on chopsticks. Then there was the main headliner, Bag of Bones Bones, a bald high yella' ninja with his belly hanging way past his belt line. He was gnawing on an unlit Havana and pacing the floor. His alligator cow boots had blazed a trail in my new Moroccan carpet. He owned a pool hall next to Angelo's dinner on the west end of Alameda Boulevard. He was everybody's fence.

I strolled over to the bar and tossed my cranberry London Fog trench over to Moe. He was already pouring me a tall Johnny Red. I lit a cigarette and filled the glass walled room with smoke.

"So what's this party about, Moe?"

"This ain't no party, sugah'," volunteered Wilma, "it's business."

I took another slow drag from my slim brown one, "Okay, so now I'm informed," I said with a little sarcasm, "What kind of business?"

Bones spoke up. His tone was gravely, like he needed to drink some water, "We're planning a bank heist, Candy."

Now' Bag of Bones was grinning at me with jagged coffee stained teeth. He was sporting an olive green three-piece. He had a wide mouth with dimples on each side. He looked like Kermit the Frog.

"Oh really!" I said, pretending to be surprised. "Any bank I know?"

"Yeah, the Hibernia, just up the street," inserted Wilma.

"You mean that little bank on Santa Clara Boulevard, that's sandwiched between Chef Chews Dinner and the 24-hour Taco joint?"

"Yeah, that's it," rallied Moe.

"Ha! You're itching for trouble, Mister, " I said with a cackle, "I wouldn't mess with a bank like that! "

"An why's that!" blasted Shotgun as though I just stepped on one of his corned foots.

I lowered my voice intentionally, almost to a whisper, "For one, the size of the bank is deceptive. Little doesn't necessarily mean easy.

Besides, it's loaded with high-tech surveillance gadgets and it's too close to home. In case you didn't know, it's got concealed commando dogs."

"BULLSHIT!" crows Shotgun Bob.

"No, she's right," counters Bones, "They're schnauzers, little shits with wiry coats, pointed ears, heavy eyebrows, and long hair on the muzzle. They ain't got no bite and very little bark, but they got an extra keen scent. They'll locate anyone, even if they're hidden in a Death Valley bunker."

"Well, how do you know so much about the Hibernia, Miss. Cane?" gruffs Shotgun rising up from the couch and posting up about an inch from my face.

"Ease-up, man," says Moe.

"I don't flinch, Mista Gun," I said with a sneer. "Your pit bull façade doesn't intimidate me. I've dealt with tricks twice your size befoe." I pressed my twin 38-C-cups up against his barrel chest. I see a gleam in his eye. He's a sissy in a man's skin, and now he and I are the only one's that know it.

"Oh yeah! Well, I ain't no Trick, woman! I could fold you up like a pretzel and stuff you in a suitcase, you smart-mouth freckled face Bitch!"

"Hold it, Shotgun. Leave my merchandise alone!" shouts Moe Betta still standing behind the bar but sliding his hand into his coat pocket like he was reaching for some heat.

I ignored Gun's derogatory comment and glanced over at Wilma. She's now seated upright. Her paisley print skirt is hiked over her chicken thighs.

"Sit down, Poppa Gun," she cooed, "I think she's on to somethin'. Let's hear the rest of what she's got to say."

"Amaretto with a lime twist!" I say to Moe. He knew the combo. It was an easy fix. He quickly hands me my drink just as Poppa Gun decides to set his big ass down. "Tricks tell me a lot of things that I'm not supposed to know. Any of you ever pull a bank job before?" They all gave me a forlorned glance. I knew the answer so I just continued with my tale, "Well, I'll make this short and sweet, amigos. I've got a hook-up, an inside track on an ex-bank teller. If you all are serious, I'll give her a call?"

Four pairs of eyes are transfixed on me as though I'm about to perform some kind of mojo or Jedi Warrior trick. So I pulled out my phone and made the call. I put it on speaker and turned up the volume. A sultry voice answered.

"Cathy's tax consulting. Corporate or otherwise, I'll save your ass some serious cash."

"Kill game, Cat. It's me Roxanne."

"Hot-damn! I was just thinkin' about callin' you. Are you done for the night?"

"Yep."

"Good, I'll be right over."

"I got company Cat and they serious. They'll need your expertise."

"A'ight, I got you. "

"And Cat…"

"Yeah…"

"Come alone."

"Gotcha!"

I looked back at my spellbound audience, "She's on her way," I assured them. Cathy Wilson is an ol' souled gangster chic. She's a natural blonde, with shoulder-length hair, big hips and big tits. She came through my doorway sportin' a black Russian fur hat and a full length burgundy sheepskin with a beautiful diamond necklace, matching bracelet, and a large pear shaped diamond ring on her pinkie finger. Her eyes were blue, almond shaped, and her skin tone exposed a beautiful tan. She looked like a dolled up white Oprah. She gave me a peck on the cheek and shook hands with everyone, even Shotgun gave her his mitt.

"My specialty is all about money, but you already know that, cause Roxanne must have told you. I got a whole lot of experience and references a mile long, "she said."

"You ever do any hard time? quizzes Bones, looking her over like he was sizing up a bucket of Church's chicken.

"Yeah, I did a 5 bit in Chowchilla back in the early nineties. What about it?"

"What for?" grumbled Shotgun.

"Fraud. Bad checks. Them were my paper hangin' days."

I didn't like the dialogue so I took control. "Enough with the twenty-one questions. She's the real deal Holyfield so just listen to what she has to say. Put 'em up on game, Cathy."

"If you need a bank to heist, well, I've got a couple in mind? What's your gimme?"

"Cash, woman! No less than half a mil!" barks Shotgun Bob.

"Okay, I got a cakewalk for ya. First Capital Bank."

"Where!" a couple voices echoed.

"Down in Sunnyvale, eight miles out. You dig?"

"I know that bank," says Moe, "It's in a shopping mall, right?"

"Shopping center, not mall. It can be easily accessed with plenty of exits."

"Will it take some heat?" asked Bones.

"Not really. Standard issue will do. I'm tellin' ya, it's cherry pie pipin hot and ready for the taking."

"How's that possible?" inquires Wilma.

"I'm in good with the lead teller. She's in the game and she'll make it easy for you."

"I still don't get it," says Shotgun cracking his knuckles.

"Look, I'll explain the rest only if you're in."

"That depends," fires Moe, "What's your take?

"Twenty-five G's. Up-front money, cash."

My face is a postage stamp. I show no emotion as I scanned the other faces in the room. Cathy's pitch for upfront money came unexpectedly. But I know Cathy. She's got em' on her hook and she's about to work 'em like a rib sandwich. "The girl that's in on it, how much she givin' up?" quizzes Moe.

"Between half a mil and three-quarters, guaranteed. She'll have you in and out in less than three minutes."

"And what's in it for her?!" snarles Gun, looking at my girl with his fake-ass pit-bull stare. He's down on his luck and he's greedy. Cathy's pitch has got everybody salivating.

"I'm in!" says Bones, breaking the icy silence in the room." I'll cover that money. So what's the plan?"

*　*　*

Saturday: 7:30 a.m.
Lawrence Road Shopping Center
Sunnyvale

I was parked along the lots perimeter fence. Shop managers were arranging displays of produce and a variety of merchandise. The First Capital Bank was scheduled to open at nine o'clock and close a little after noon. But there was a problem. At four a.m. a fog bank crept inland and settled in the South Bay. It was thick. It looked like the kind that would hang around for a while.

My girls were already on the scene. Disguised in blue cover-alls and matching caps, no one paid them any attention as one squeegeed window fronts and the other pushed a cart carrying a trash can and janitorial supplies. At eight o'clock sharp, the bank manager and lead teller arrived just as Shotgun and Moe Betta pulled up in a white Ford Econoline van. Dressed in gray business suits and black cordovan shoes, they flashed their fake security billfold badges and ushered the pair of employees through the first set of doors.

In the lobby, I saw Moe spray paint the lens of camera number one. Beyond that, there was nothing more to see.

* * *

"GET ON THE FLOOR!" shouted Shotgun Bob, aiming a short handled sawed off at the manager's head, "Hit them cameras with paint, Moe!"

Now seriously frightened, the lead teller raised both hands in the air.

"What you lookin' at?!" snarled Shotgun, "Ain't you supposed to make this easy!"

"Ya-yeah-yeah, sure...the cart, everything is behind the vault cage, in the cart," she said pointing shakily towards the rear of the bank's spacious room.

"The keys are in my pocket," muffled the manager, still lying spread eagle on the cold linoleum floor.

The lead teller stood frozen. Her eyes were luminous like a deer trapped in headlights.

"Get the keys, woman!" commanded Moe, "Let's go! Let's go!"

"MOVE!" shouted Shotgun.

The teller unlocked the cage, grabbed the cart, and rolled it out to where Shotgun still had the manager at bay.

"How do you get this thang open?!" cried Moe, trying to use his physical strength.

Still trembling and in a panic, the teller reached under the cart and triggered a switch and the cart's steel lid clicked open.

Moe lifted the lid, "Oooh, look-ah-here!"

"We wastin' time, Moe. Examine the shit and make sure it's real."

Moe and Shotgun we're looking at bricks and bricks of currency, sealed in clear plastic, six inches thick, rows of crisp Jefferson's and Franklin's, just staring back at the two-bit gangsters. The men laughed like hyenas as the bank manager yelped.

"The silent alarm has been tripped. She failed to use the proper unlocking sequence!"

Both men glared at the teller.

"Dumb-ass, bitch!"

"LET'S ROLL!"

* * *

Once again, I watched as they burst through the bank's swinging door, and loaded their cargo into the van. Moments later, they streaked past my parked car. I waited as their tail-lights vanished in the fog. Shortly after, my girls rolled their cart in line with First Capital's entrance door. I witnessed several hefty trash bags slam dunked into the canister. We met up in an alley, directly behind the shops and stuffed the bags in the trunks of two separate cars. Then we caravanned eastbound down the Lawrence expressway, and as the police sirens grew nearer and nearer we oozed into the traffic's freeway.

* * *

"Slow down, Shotgun!" cried Moe, who kept checking the side view mirror, "It ain't wise to be speedin' in fog."

"Take a chill pill, Moe. I'll ease up as soon as I get past this next diesel."

"Sure, sure," says Moe grinning yet still paranoid, "But why the rush? I already knew you never intended to show up at Candy's pad with the loot. But, what about Bones? Are you going to sting him too? I don't think-"

"Look, Moe! Let me do the thinking, okay. You just keep watch and make sure no patrol cars sneak up on us. Besides, we are some rich-ass motha's."

"Hell-yeah! I'd say with the heft of that cart, it's definitely more than half-a-million."

"Ha-ha, don't worry yourself, son. Once we get settled up in Vancouver, Bones ain't gonna bother us 'cause were gonna' send him twice as much as much he was expecting."

* * *

No one knows for certain why the Highway patrolman forced the white Ford van to pull over. All I know is somebody panicked. Moe used a thirty gauge sawed-off to take out the patrol car's radiator and front right tire. I read that the unsuspecting cop was so frightened that he never had a chance to draw his holstered gun. I suspect with Shotgun behind the wheel he must have put the pedal to the metal and tried to get past one of them road hoggin diesels. But with the fog being so thick they smacked head-on into another semi-truck. At least that's how the newspaper read. Witnesses reported that the van's gas tank exploded on impact. A crime scene detective said the vans chassis and two skeletal remains were burned to a crisp. The banks money had incinerated, and the metal cart was demolished.

All of us, Cathy Wilson, Wilma Sarpy, Bag of Bones Bones and myself, certainly weren't surprised. I knew that they couldn't be trusted with the real dough so that's why I orchestrated the heist the way I did, making sure that they took the counterfeit bills and my girls took the real cash. If they, Moe and Shotgun Bob, would've kept it 100 and made it back to my condo to divvy-up the loot, then I would've split the real cash with them, as planned. But Thank God momma didn't raise no fool. It's like she once said…'child it's sting or be stung'.

In chess, thinking ahead, several moves at a time, usually leads to winning the game. Well, in life, it's the same way. But instead of losing your queen or your king, you may lose your head. This time though, the sting-ees got stung…Check-mate!

* * *

ROXXY

CHAPTER TWO

Elmwood

March 14th
Elmwood Correctional
Facility Milpitas California

IT'S MY BIRTHDAY, an' despite these gloomy surroundings, I'm just glad to be alive to see twenty-five. At 5:00 a.m. a pot-bellied guard tapped my bottom bunk and ordered me to rise. I peered from under the four layers of sheets and blankets at a pale stretch of nothin' but neck. His golf ball-sized Adams apple throbbed with every syllable he spat.

"Get ready for court house transport. I'm giving you 45 minutes," he mewed, looking like Sylvester cat after he just swallowed Tweety Bird. I wasn't loving it. I hadn't slept much last night and now my stomach was cramped. However, a hot and steamy shower with twelve shower heads all to myself improved my mood.

After the First Capital Bank heist everything was peachy keen for a while, like about eight or nine months. I took my share of the six-way split and invested about 30 thousand into an antique store. It was a girlfriend's business in the Old Town section of Los Gatos. Most of what remained went into a trust with Esquire Karrene Cash. She came highly recommended. She built her reputation in family law before

18

switching over to criminals. But just to cut through the chase, that's why I prefer to work alone, 'cause when you got crime'ees or co-defendants, someone is certain to fuck up.

My weak link was the bank manager, a dude from Belize. He was told never to make any large cash purchases and no extravagant vacations for at least a year. However, his wife was going through chemo, so he used some of his stash to pay off an expensive medical bill. Then came 'The Watchers'. The surveillance team were watchin' and the pros came into play. Unsavory FBI types we're sitting in the shadows, chain smoking and eye-balling me through a telescopic leans.

As I was sayin', the banker was first on the FBI's hit list. They taunted him with pictures of faces, places, and cars. Finally, he whined like a politician who'd just been caught on film for smoking crack. The rest of us didn't go down so easily. We were all well experienced with the long arm of the law. We had a few tricks up our sleeves. Nobody blabbed so nobody got hurt.

The charge was fraud and conspiracy to commit fraud but it had no legs. They couldn't prove a robbery charge, so they immediately threw that out as well. As for me, I was the least likely to be considered a ring leader, and the Feds didn't know anything about me because I didn't have a record. No spikes and no strikes, except that I'm now caught up in this creep show shit.

A fireman rescue team found me tapped out on the living room carpet of a friend's apartment. I vaguely remember patches of blurred images. It was like a dream within a dream. Have you ever gone to sleep and had a dream and within that dream your asleep and having another dream?

Well, I know it makes no sense, but it happened to me.

* * *

I was lying in the front seat of my Lexus. My legs were too long, so my driver's side door was flung open. The engine was still running and the garage door was shut. I didn't smell gas. I didn't smell exhaust. Twice my eyelids fluttered and I could see the clock display. It read 3:00 a.m. I tried to move. The slightest twitch felt like I had been doused in corn syrup. My arms were noodles. My legs were stitched together with sawdust pouring out. I thought I was a balloon in a Macy's Day Parade. I stared at the keys in the ignition for what seemed to be like a very long time. Then I shut my eyes tight like that chick in "Bewitched", and suddenly the engine shut off. I was standing, spinning, and falling. Falling like a Christmas tree that's got no way to protect itself from an accidental tip. My heart stopped. I tried to grab my face because it was about to be smashed. Then came a jolt. My heart had done a reboot.

My eyes opened. Six gangly lookin' people were standing over me. They were firemen and medical techs. My breath smelled like vomit. My pants suit was urine soaked. I was laid out on a carpet, drenched in a pool of champagne. Four pairs of spider monkey hands lifted me up as they strapped me in a gurney. I felt the rumble of asphalt and a siren's wail.

* * *

Minutes turned into hours and hours into days. Eventually, I regained my strength and was able to talk. My voice is raspy. My throat felt like it had been reamed with some obscene object. A Filipino nurse in a lilac colored uniform was checking me out.

"What you lookin' at?" I managed to grovel.

"Oh, good morning, Ms. Blackwell. How are you feeling...better?"

She shellacked me with large black pupils and a shit-eatin' grin. "Is that all you got to say? How about askin' me if I'm hungry, 'cause I could eat a whole pig right about now."

She giggles, "Ooou, you're a wild one, Ms. Blackwell. Here, let me adjust your bed."

The nurse grabbed the remote from a bedside table and my mattress snakes forward. I'm now in an upright position with my ashy freckled arms folded across my bosom. I'm glaring at her like she's despicable and I'm expecting Ritz Carlton room service. But it doesn't seem to faze her. She's still grinning as she prances off and returns within a matter of seconds with a breakfast tray on wheels. I wanted to inhale the entire tray. The aromas were scrumptiously delicious. Western egg omelet, hash browns, marmalade on buttered toast, freshly baked pastrami strips, and three shots of them pure orange juice cups.

During the time it took me to wolf down my brunch, Nurse Joy, that's what her name tag said, had pulled up a stool and chose to smile at me. So I put my fork to rest, curled my lip like Elvis, and belched. Once again, Nurse Joy cuffed her left hand over her mouth and giggled. I watched her climb down from the stool like she was a midget and then she attempted to relieve me of my tray. I had a vice grip on it and snatched it back.

"Did I say I was done, Nurse Joy!"

She gave me bug-eyes and shook her wide forehead until a mane of jet black hair came loose and fell to her shoulders.

"I'm cool," I finally said with a smirk, "you can take my tray now!"

With caution, she gently removed the tray and gave me a tiny bow.

"Oh, and one more thing before you go."

"Yes, Ms. Blackwell."

"What the hell is this?" I said yanking the covers from the foot of my bed and exposing my left leg.

Nurse Joy frowned and squinched her button nose, "Oh, that. That's an ankle bracelet, Ms. Blackwell. Everyone in this Wing is under sheriff's protective custody."

"Custody? For what!" I barked.

"For your suicide attempt. You overdosed on someone else's medication and the doctor found traces of cocaine in your system."

"Suicide?"

"Ah-yes, it's on your chart."

"Cocaine?"

Nurse Joy nods her head up and down as though she's afraid to utter another word. I'm puzzled but I haven't gotten a clear head yet. I'm wondering like, "What the hell?" I don't have a cocaine habit. I'm not addicted to nothin' except maybe sex. Although I do know I'm having dreams that don't make any sense, an' if the man upstairs is trying to tell me somethin'…then I wish he'd hurry the hell up and let me in on the secret.

* * *

So once again, I'm in the shower stall playin' with a bar of soap and feelin' up my pussy, 'cause I ain't had none since God knows when. But I do have something to look forward to according to my lawyer. Esquire Karren is one of them cooper tone flavored lookin' sistas about five-nine, with long stems just like me. She got that Jamaican shag thing goin' wih the hair. My girl, Cat, says her family is rich. They oughta' be, because her fees are costing me some serious bands.

It didn't take but a sec for me and a couple other girls to get dressed and cuffed. We weren't high escape risk so nobody got shackled.

Once we were seated on the cold-ass jail house bus, this big butt white girl was the first to blab.

"Bus driver! Put some heat on in this mutha' fucka'. We aint from Alaska, don't cha' know."

I had to laugh. She'd just washed her hair and it stank up the whole bus, but the bitch was funny. The bus driver cranks the engine and lets it idle for about ten minutes. We're feeling a little more comfy now but we're anxious to get going, and now the driver is reading a newspaper.

"Hey, yoouu-whhoo! Dude!" yells that fat white girl. "What are you doing, waiting for the police escort? You are the police, remember, so let's go."

The driver chuckles, "Hold on to your undies, girlie. Today you're riding with company," he says as he glances at his watch, "and they'll be here in just a bit."

Now, the three of us girls are exchanging blank stares wondering…who in the hell? When suddenly there's shouts and hoots coming up the rear side of the bus. It's men! Gay men. There's about a dozen of them, and they all think they're cute. Some are wearing fake-ass lipstick from Kool-Aid packs. Others were dippin' and switchin' like they got real pussy between their legs. They're a multi-cultural mix, six whites, two Asians and four blacks. The black transgender men were naturally the loudest of the set but not necessarily the most flamboyant. I could tell by their hips and tits that some where taking hormones.

I sat up-front, opposite the bus driver's booth. Two of the gay men chose seats directly across from me. One was sienna brown and obese with big white Colgate teeth. He introduced himself.

"They call me Ronnie, love."

"My pleasure, I'm Roxanne," I replied as we reached across the aisle and touched fingertips like some type of pimpish ritual. The other guy was caramel colored and petite. He just gazed at me with a doe-like expression. He reminded me of "Bambi". He was definitely cute. Pencil thin mustache, hair done up in something resembling a finger wave which was parted to the left side of his peanut shaped scalp. There was a tiny jewel piercing on the left side of his nose.

Ronnie couldn't sit still. His plump ass was perched on the edge of his seat, "This is Miss. Kenny, Roxanne," said Ronnie like he was a game show host displaying some merchandise up for a bid. I was timing him to see how long it would take him to shut his mouth.

Miss. Kenny was eye-balling me like he was sizing up his competition. Then he slayed me with a child-like smile. "Oooo!" I thought to myself, this little tease has got some game. He probably ain't having no problem getting some old geezer's pecker to stand up. Ron was into boys, young teenage, white boys. Barely legal as some folks called them. Kenny was rich. He was a minister's son. His family owned a cable station up in Fairfield and a whole lot of California real estate.

Neither man had a dope habit, but they weren't squeaky clean either. Miss. Kenny like showin' out, flossing and partying. He threw away money like he had a basement full of it. His ching-a-ling was stealing his mother's credit cards, and on occasion, dressing up like her. She kept having to throw him in jail which was a feeble attempt to break his rebellious trip. Kenny was spoiled badly and had a reputation of hanging out with old Rich farts who'd lavish him with expensive gifts.

"Yeah, Miss. Kenny likes to wear his momma's clothes," egged Ronnie.

"Quit telling her my business, Ronnie! That's ugly. If she was interested, she'd have asked."

"Oh, I'm interested, Miss. Kenny. Why don't you give me your version?"

Kenny straightened up like a letter 'L' and put those big fawn eyes on me, "You said your name is Roxanne?"

"That's right, surgah'."

"Well, you can start getting to know me by just calling me Kenny. Leave the 'Missy' part out because that's Ronnie's Simple Simon way of talking and putting funny little labels on people. "

Ronnie giggles like he enjoys hearing Kenny criticize him, and Kenny's got a little kid's voice. He sounds like Elmo.

"Of course I'm gay, but I'm not trying to pass myself off as a woman," continues Kenny, "I like being a man." Kenny's dark browns look past me as if he's reading from a teleprompter. "Yes, I role play a little because it works to my advantage. Unlike Ronnie, who's little pea-shooter never gets hard unless he's got one in his mouth."

"Ooou, Miss. Dragon Breath, stop," wooed Ronnie unabashed.

"Oh, but I'm not finished with you, you lard-ass Hostess Twinkie. Roxanne, you see that wet spot on his smock?"

"I do-what is it?" I instigate.

"That's Ronnie's milk duds. When he gets excited his nipples leak just like a woman's."

"Like a real woman," says Ronnie, "because I'm a woman in a man's body," he replied, striking a pose and doing her version of a Wendy Williams palm flip.

"Ooou, you've got gynecomastia," I tease.

"Huh?"

"That means your titties are lactating."

"Whatever you say, Roxanne, 'cause it sounds sexy to me." He finishes by snapping his fingers and waiving a handcuffed right hand through the air.

"So now it's your turn, Roxanne. What got you here because you don't look or act like an average jail house diva?"

"I'm here, because the Law froze my account and I couldn't bail out."

"Drug beef, sales I bet," meddled Ronnie.

"Nah, nothing like that. Let's just say, they think I'm going to lead them onto something big, but I've got a good lawyer, Honey, and I should be released sometime today."

"What's his name?" asked Ronnie.

"It's not a him it's a her. Cash, Karrene Cash."

"I know a Cash," volunteered Ronnie. "His name is Houston. He hooks me up with a lot of quality clients."

"Clients?"

"Yeah, Bubble-lips is an auto mechanic," volunteers Kenny.

"That's right," says Ronnie, his fat lips drooling as he strokes his close-cut bowling ball head like he's just stepped out of a beauty salon. "And, I'm very good at what I do, Honey. I'm like a splash of perfume fragrance that's unforgettable."

"Shut up, Ronnie!" blast Kenny, "Because everybody knows you really do stink!"

The two men are silly and keep me laughing during the entire ride. We exchange cell phone numbers and we're each taken to separate courthouses for the business at hand.

* * *

I ended up at the superior court building on North First Street in downtown San Jose. It sat on the corner opposite Saint James Park. Me and the sheriff escort rode the lobby elevator to the 14th floor. The hallway entrance was jammed with men and women in business suits carrying briefcases. It was supposed to be my arraignment but my lawyer had evidently pulled another rabbit from under her skirt. Karrene bobbed and weaved past a dozen suits. She was decked-out in Abercrombie and Finch. The guard un-cuffed me as we ducked through a side door and entered a room that was not much bigger than a walk-in closet.

"How you doin', Roxanne?"

"I'm doin'. How you doin'?" I arch my eye-brows as I tagged her back, "cause you lookin' like a million-bucks," I razzled.

"Tru-dat." She smiles and cocks her pointy chin to one side and flashes me a row or pearly whites, "I got some good news and some even better news, but it all depends on you."

"You can miss me with the intrigue and suspense, Karrene, just give it to me straight."

"Okay, fine. The D.A. is skipping a prelim but he wants to cut a deal and the judge is in our court on this."

"Okay," I say with a little trepidation in my voice as Karrene continues with her jibber jabber. I'm squinting my right eye thinking this chick must have not heard a word I just said.

"If you agree," she warbles, "this judge is going to release you on your own recognizance to do an outpatient drug program for ninety days."

"What? An' outpatient program?"

"There's no need to be upset, Roxanne. The D.A. has agreed to unfreeze your account and you'll be released by noon."

"Just like that?"

"Yes, just like that, but…"

"I knew there'd be a but!" I rolled up the sleeves of my smock because I'm really pissed about doing the program.

"Stop right there!" quakes Karrene. She leans into my face. She's tougher than I thought. If I had any thoughts about boo-boppin' this chick…well, it's obvious she ain't about to let it happen.

"Take the deal, Ms. Blackwell."

 Karrene and I are about the same height. We're eye-to-eye and there's something about her body language that's turning me on. But I don't need some chick sucking on my ass and clit' right now. Of course I'm horny, but what I really want is some dick. So I give my lawyer some breathing room, "let's get on with this," I say, "because I'm dying for a cigarette."

She winks, reaches inside her blazer pocket, and slides a fresh pack of non-filtered generics, and I quickly stuff them in my waist band.

My brief encounter with the magistrate was a breeze. She was another pretty O.G. lesbian chick who was running her mouth at warp speed and in full lust mode. She layed a gazzilion questions on me and I had to politely answer, Yes, your honor,' and "No, your honor," about fifty times.

* * *

CHAPTER THREE

My Lai
(ME LIE)

Santa Clara County Booking
Mission Street, San Jose, CA
High noon

"So tell me, Esquire Karrene, when is the D.A. gonna unfreeze my accounts?"

"Try practicing a little patience, Ms. Blackwell. Trust me, it will do wonders for your stress level."

I try slaying her with snake eyes, but she just keeps on chirping, "It's going to take a couple of days."

"A couple of days? What's so hard about a simple phone call to the bank."

"I'll look into it, okay, but don't go 51-50 on me."

"Karrene flips open her attaché and digs out a check book.

"How much will you need to get by?"

"Oh about 50,000."

She shirks me with a smirk and tosses her checkbook back into her case.

"I'm just kidding. Can't you take a joke?"

Karrene sighs and gives me one of those, I've had enough of your stares.

"My bad," I say, "no problem. I may have a little something stashed in my apartment. Let me use your phone for a sec." She reopened her briefcase, hands me her phone and I immediately make a call.

"Hey, Cathy! It's me, Roxanne! How's my Mugsy?"

"It's about time you called somebody, Roxanne. Mugsy is fine. He gobbles up everything I cook."

"You're not supposed to cook for a dog, Cathy. You're supposed to feed him dog food. Retail pet food is a big business in case you didn't know."

"There you go with the sarcasm. He's an ugly fat bastard of a pit, but he's sweet. Did you teach him how to hump people's legs when he has to take a piss?"

"How dare you poke fun at my dog, Cathy. I ain't havin it. I had to housebreak him the best way I knew, cuz I'm not about to let a mutt ruin my Persian rugs no matter how much I like him."

"Excuuuse me. By the way, are you calling from a calaboose?"

"Yeah, I'm still in police custody, but I'm using my lawyer's phone. I'll soon be signing my release papers. So Cathy, tell me something... Is that surveillance team still hanging out in your hood?"

"I haven't seen any signs of 'em lately, but I see no evil and I ain't heard none--"

"Kill game, Cat. It's a cell phone. Besides, we both know you were born with a criminal's mind."

"Hush, girl, be nice. So, when are you coming by?

"Soon, like this evening around six-ish. Put some Pink Chablis on ice, and if you got time, hook us up something special,"

"You want real food or take out?"

"Ribs, baby. Slay me a slab of beef."

"Hibachi style?"

"Yeah, hickory smoke that sucka'."

"Gottcha."

"I gotta run, Cat, cuz my mouthpiece is frowning at me and tapping her watch like my time is up or something. Arrivederci Baby."

*　*　*

When I arrived at my penthouse it had this musty-ass smell so I opened the veranda's sliding glass doors to air everything out. Afterwards, I switched on a 'Sade' playlist. The surround system sounded smooth. Then I went to the fridge and liberated a wad of cash that was stashed in the freezer compartment, stuffed between some chicken breasts. I made a spread on my dinette table and let the cold cash thaw. Then I got a warm oil bath going and oozed myself in. "Ooou-shit", ain't nothing that feels as good as hot slick oil tantalizing my crevices.

I rolled a blunt from my stash-box and fired up, then immediately snuffed it out. The weed was too dry. I needed to pick up a fresh supply. I made a mental note, closed my eyes, and my mind went wandering...

My thoughts went to Ronnie and Miss. Kenny. They were hilarious. Kenny invited me to his home coming bash, somewhere up in Berkeley. He said it was going to be a poolside garden party. I told him if my schedule permitted I'd make it my business to be there. To my surprise, Karrene was a friend of his family and had planned to attend. Apparently she was an alumni of Cal-Berkley and the reigning president of a sorority. The bitch had clout. She asked me to be her date, so I agreed. But Ronnie's big lips is what really had me trippin'. They was all juicy and bubbly with every word he spoke, similar to a baby's drool. I think that must come from sucking a lot of dick. In my line of business, I ain't gotta do a lot of suckin', because when I shake my money-maker my clients shoot in a blink. Sometimes they already done blinked on themselves before we even get started. I can get a man to blink between my titties and most blink between my legs, 'cause I get 'em so worked up they can't tell the difference between clam shut thighs and a real pussy. So what a chick really needs to do is drain a man of his strength and keep the power, Baby.

Some chicks are sick or just plain mean. They want to see a client suffer, not for gamesmanship sake, they're just hateful. They despise the trick for a variety of reasons. Maybe they got a manager who's been messin' over them, or puttin' hands on 'em. Or maybe they keep flashing back on some relative who abused them when they were too young to defend themselves. I'm not saying it's a way to be, but it is what it is. A chick has got to find a way to justify the errors of a cruel world. And I'll admit, I've been lucky so far.

Nevertheless, I like to bring a man a treat, by adding a little sparkle to his life, and putting some stacks in my bank account. He'll remember me by the feel good stuff I do. That way, he be begging to see me again and again. And that's when I jack up my price scale and shorten my sessions. I like a client to be salavatin' when he thinks of me.

Ooou...and one more thing. I'm not into that kinky shit, because that can be dangerous. I'll let a monk suck my toes or lick my crevices, but he better not try and kiss me. I'm serious! If he crosses the line, I immediately check out, because if he wants to see me again, he's got to play by my rules.

Sometimes I run across a client who really knows what he's doing. He knows all the right buttons to tweak on a woman's body. You know, all the g-spots. You got to work fast with a client like that. You'd best hide your emotions, because they're the type that be trying to flip game on you.

Now if a chick looking to get out of the game and find herself a steady rock, then it's cool. But, if you wanna stay independent, its best you keep the power, baby. Turn him on and make sure he get his nutt. Slip a finger up his booty while you suck on his dick. They be loving it! A little torture brings ecstasy, I guess. And teasing is legit. It just makes the memories of them lame tricks go away and completely forgettable...

ROXXY

* * *

I'm getting out of the tub 'cause my body is starting to look like a prune. I guess I lost track of time. My mind is clouded with too many thoughts. I was still a little damp, so I tip-toed back to my living room. The cold cash was completely thawed. By the time it took to towel myself dry, I realized I needed more cash, like a good grip, a hundred stacks or bettter. An OG once told me, "Roxanne, don't get caught up by making one too many moves, think it through. Get a clear picture of your end game."

Well, most of what he said sunk in but not right away. Sometimes, I allowed spontaneity to run me ragged. Like most people, I had to do things my way until I finally figured out how to apply what the OG actually meant.

The one thing about investing money in a friend's business is that the cash is not always at your fingertips when you need it. Bills come first. Plus, I had maxed out my credit cards. Then it dawned on me that I had a client who's a money broker. His name was Bill, Nasty Bill. All Bill liked to do was suck pussy. The problem was he wasn't any good at it, so I always charged him an outrageous price. Bill never seemed to mind the price, so I gave him a call...

"Security Escrow and Equity, may I help you?" answered a girl with a sweet adolescent voice.

"I'd like to speak to Bill Muldune."

"Whom should I say is calling, please?"

"Tell 'em its Roxanne, surgah'."

"Ah, okay."

There's about a minute wait before a bombastic voice comes blaring over the phone, "B. Muldune speaking! How may I be of service?"

"I like you better when you're less formal and not so loud, Bill. I can hear real good in case you didn't know."

Bill lowers his voice, as he apparently cupped one hand over the receiver, "Easy, Candy Girl. I'm breaking in a newbie, and she's only been with me for a week. I still need to make a good impression."

"Oh, I know what that means."

"What?"

"Un-huh, pink muffin with or without the whipped cream."

"Cut it out, Blackwell. Unlike you, I don't mix business with pleasure."

"Sure you're right, Mr. Slobber Lips."

"Okay, so you got some new jokes. I don't even want to know who you borrowed that from. So what's really on your mind? You need some capital?"

"Bingo! Hell-yeah, I want to invest in a little somethin'."

"Like what, you know I got a smorgasbord of goodies."

"You still pushing those certificates?"

"Yeah, I got some Jumbos available, if you can cover the interest?"

"A Jumbo?"

"Yep."

"Hmm...I've heard about them. What's my limit?"

"How about a hundred thou for starters?"

I whistle..."Okay, so slap me with some cheese, Nigga."

"Huh?"

"The terms, what are the terms?"

"Oh, you provide me with the down, twelve percent and I'll make a call to a bank manager of your choice and have the bond wire transferred over. Then you can use the funds for whatever purpose you chose but the face value of the certificate must be replaced to your account in eighteen months, otherwise, heavy penalties will be levied against you and me."

"Damn you, Nasty Bill! I'm not a corporation, Dude."

"Don't forget, the economy just took a heavy hit, and it's still on the rebound. You want the deal or not?"

I didn't have a better option and I had a jones for some serious cash, "Let's deal. Citi Bank, Cupertino branch, the manager's name is—"

"David Mateen, yes, I know him. Now, I'm only going to be in my office until three this afternoon. Can you meet me down at the Interlude around four?

"The Interlude? Oh, you're talking about the downtown diner on the corner of West Santa Clara and Third?"

"Yeah, that's the one."

"Okay, Bill, but I've got an' impatient caller on hold. I'll see you around four."

"Roxanne here, talk to me cuz I do talk back!"

A gruff voice laughs and I recognize the laugh. Its Bag of Bones-Bones.

"Bones, I was just about to text you," I said with good cheer, "you must of read my mind."

Bones cackles, "Good to hear your voice, Roxxy. It's almost as though you just rose back from the dead. How was your first trip to the tank?"

"You mean the fish bowl, fool. And it wasn't anything like in the movies, in case you've forgotten. We'll swap jailhouse tales later. Right now I need you to front me a ten spot."

"You runnin' a little short?"

"Something like that, but you must know that I prefer to spend other people's money. Its principle, you know what I'm sayin'."

"Well, I got principles too, and my policy is I ain't giving nothin' up unless I'm getting something in return."

"Ha, as if I didn't know that. So you got something lined up and you need me and my girls."

"That's right. While you been layin' up and eatin' shit on the shingle—"

"Excuse me, its cream chipped beef over burnt toast. Apparently your reprobate mind has forgotten."

Bones laughs heartily. He takes a while to catch his breath, "You're insane, woman. But this is square business, because I got us a monster hit."

"Oh yeah, well it sounds like you've been smokin' some monster rocks."

"Forget about it...What's today, Tuesday?"

"All day."

"Well, that's perfect. Our little caper can go down Friday night. So clear your calendar we'll have a meet. How's tonight?

"I'm busy. Cathy and I are planning a little celebration at her place."

"Not a good idea, 'cause Cat's place is probably bugged, and I ain't got time to perform a sweep. Transport the party to your place. Wilma and I will come by around eight."

"Suit yourself, Bones, but all bullshit aside, this one betta' be a damn good fix."

"Oh, it's a gem. I guarantee it."

"By the way, when can I get my peanuts?"

"I'll get the kid, Tommy Boy, to drop it off within the hour. It will be gift wrapped in your favorite colors."

"Oh-really, and what colors might that be?"

"A crisp green and white with a red seal running through it."

* * *

Like clockwork, Tommy Boy delivered my package. Gift wrapped in my favorite colors was ten thousand dollars. I put on some running gear and jogged over to the Interlude. By four-thirty, Nasty Bill and I downed a couple glasses of suds. While we were chit-chatting I checked the status of the wire transfer from my phone. Touchdown! I was one-hundred thousand dollars richer just like that. Upon my return to Terra Cotta Heights, my doorman was standing at attention with Mugsy at his side. Mugsy humped my leg and when the elevator door jerked open, he leaped into my arms, then the two of us rode up to our hutch. I didn't see Cathy but signs of her were everywhere. Every condiment and spice was laid out on my kitchen counter. A smoky hue clung to the ceiling of my living room. We were having guests so she had ribs in the kitchen's range broiler as well as the hibachi on the terrace.

Mugsy sniffed Cathy out while she was doing her business in the guest bathroom. I put on a nice play list - Amy Winehouse and an American Gangster sound track.

By the time I finished showering, I slipped into a set of burgundy sweats and pink house shoes. I was about to pour myself a glass of Pink Chablis when Wilma and Bones showed up. They were early, tipsy, and clowning. They had an Asian girl with them who looked like the actress, Lucy Liu, and Wilma was strapped to Bones hip like she'd been taking lessons from Mugsy. Bones and Wilma were decked out in the latest thug-wear, khakis, pendeltons, and suede's. They were all sporting hats. Bones, a felt fedora, and Wilma wore a candy apple Panamanian bolero. It was hella cute. And the Asian chick, named My Lai, pronounced "Me Lie", which meant mixed race, she wore an apple green beanie, green jeans, jeweled clogs, and a canary yellow hoody that had the word "Tiger" stenciled on the left sleeve and some Asian script on the right.

"Ya'll bring something to add to this party!" snorted Cathy looking bug eyed in a chef's apron holding a fork in one hand and a spatula in the other.

Bag of Bone-Bones, set a shopping bag on the counter. He was chewing on the nub of an unlit Cuban cigar and switched it from one corner of his mouth to the other, "Yeah, we bought some brew-skis and little nip."

The liquor was a pint of Hennessy and a bottle of Remy Martin, his favorites and nobody else's. The aroma from Cathy's grill skills had impregnated the room. Everyone was famished so we all chipped in. Bones did a slice and dice with tomatoes, bell peppers, cucumber, and fresh light green chili peppers.

Wilma helped me make the Q-sauce—wine vinegar, cilantro, garlic, rosemary, and thymes mixed with a can of Las Palmas chili mix and a can of tomato paste. We added a splash of ketchup and a shot of Tabasco.

My Lai impressed me with her willingness to pitch in. She made a pitcher of a drink called "Moo Tai", a Chinese rum and coke mix, but since we had neither, she improvised using papaya juice and some cognac. Up to that point, I didn't know much about her but I found out later that she was an ex Afghan Combat Vet.

Just prior to glazing the steaks and ribs with Q-sauce, I pulled out two trays of baked potato skins from my oven. The Fab-Five of us chowed down like a bevy of hungry crocodiles as we discussed Ponsi schemes in between bites. Bones was about to give us the particulars to his ambitious heist when Wilma cut him off.

"Hey, Roxxy, how'd you do in court? Did the judge give you twenty-minutes-to-life?"

"Suck a donkey dick, Wilma," I yammered with angst pretending to mean it.

I sort of liked Wilma but she was quick to get stuck on stupid when she drank. Trying to contain her was to no avail, cuz' everybody was already laughing at the two of us and giving her back-talk was like inviting her to punish you with her arsenal of jokes. Then she got up from the couch and stood in the middle of my living room floor and did a sultry shimmy. She was thrusting her hips about a foot in each direction, and in a high-pitched voice she said – 'Come inside my cell and let me be your woman for a day, said the sleazy rat-faced morphadite to the young and tender fish that just hit the line. I'll let you do my helmet if you let me squeeze your ass.'

No one could hold back a burst of laughter and neither could I. This olive-oil, chicken thighed bitch was hilarious. She needed to be on stage at the comedy club. Bones was eatin' it up. He just had to egg her on.

"How big was that morphadite's penis, Wilma?"

"That chick's dick was no bigger than my pinky toe!" she screeched.

"What makes you think your toe is pink, woman?" gibed Bones.

"Humph, my toe may not be pink, but my pussy is and I keep it shaved tighter than five Gillette blades."

Bones couldn't trip her, and everyone knew they were tossing each other up in the bedroom.

"Enough with your extrapolating, woman, let's main-line some coffee and get down to business. Me Lie, it's your turn to take the mic. What can you tell us about this caper?"

My Lai took a sip of Moo Tai and cracked her knuckles, "I work for Brinks. I'm an armored car driver. I use to be into code-breaking, in special forces training. Brinks don't pay much and it's dangerous work. And since I'm going in and out of banks every day, I came up with an idea. I got on the internet and broke through some bank codes and I moved cash from one account to another. I waited a few days and went back in and the money was still listed under the wrong accounts, just as I had arranged them. I used a friend's account number and stored the money in hers. The next day she made a withdrawal and closed out the account."

"How much did she withdraw?" asked Cat.

"Ten thousand dollars."

"Okay, so let me get this straight," challenged Wilma. "You switched the accounts in one bank, or did you switch money from two different banks?"

"First, I did a switch within the bank. Like, one Wells Fargo branch, then later, I got wiser and switched from one branch to another branch in different locations. I ran the scam for about four months. The hardest part was finding people who I could trust to rent me use of their accounts. Then I read about a case in New York of a guy who got busted using a system similar to mine."

"So what did you do, quit?" quaked Wilma.

"That's right. I did a couple more hits and shut it down."

I'm just kicking back as I watch the two girls shoot a barrage of questions at My Lai. She's confident and smart.

"What was your take?" asked Cathy.

My Lai sucked her teeth, "I made about four hundred thousand for myself, minus what I paid out to the account holders."

"The partners?"

"Right, the partners."

"Oh, so you wanna broaden your scheme and go for a big score?"

stated Wilma displaying a bit of attitude. I could tell she was jealous of My Lai's daring.

"No, that's not true. It was too risky. I had to use different computers at coffee shops and libraries to avoid being tracked. Then I started sorting through business accounts and found what at first glance appeared to be a small company called Echo Systems. Their specialty was dealing in synthetic gem stones, powdered gold, and imported diamonds. According to their docket numbers they were taking in nine million worth of diamond imports a year for about five years."

"I know a little somethin' about the diamond exchange business," interrupted Cathy, crossing and re-crossing her calves. That was a sign she was getting excited. "But what was the powdered gold used for?"

"Electroplating," said Bones. "You don't need to be a rocket scientist to figure that. This is Silicon Valley, in case you forgot."

"He's right," added My Lai. "The powdered gold is a major product used by companies that produce semiconductors and printed circuitry."

"Okay, so who's the owner of Echo Systems and where are they located?" shot Wilma anxious to move the conversation along and get to the point.

"Well, that's where I ran into a problem. There is no plant or warehouse business address because the company folded and supposedly liquidated all it's assets. However, the name 'Hash Patel' was listed as the company's president, so I did a Google search and found nearly a dozen Patel's listed in the U.S., but only a few were living on the West Coast. They owned several properties mostly underdeveloped real estate, a few South Bay apartment buildings, and a Thrift and Drug Variety Store in the city of Campbell."

"Oh, you mean that suburb that's south of San Jo?" said Wilma.

"Un-huh, that's right," replied My Lai finally picking up on Wilma's impatient vibe.

"A Drug Thrift Store!" added Cathy.

"Yeah, I found it odd as well, but I figured if Hash Patel didn't liquidate everything he owned, then he probably still had a stash of diamonds, and the thrift store might be the perfect place to store them."

I watch as My Lai stares back at Bones. She's done talking. Bones clears his throat and takes a slug of cognac straight from the bottle, "It's like this ladies—it's an unlikely place but I've got some inside info that says the stash does exist and its being kept in a room next to a walk-in cooler."

"You're kidding!" shouts Wilma, practically falling off of the stool. After drinking half a bottle of Remy Martin, her bloodshot-eyes were almost shut. "You mean the place in stores where you see racks of beer and sodas behind frosty glass doors?"

"Yeah, something like that," said Bones as he snatches the bottle of Remy away from her. "It's a storage room and it's packed with five gallon opaque plastic containers. The typical non-descript type, sealed so tight that you may have to use a crowbar or claw hammer just to pry open the lids."

"So I'm supposing everything is wired and burglar proof, right?" asked Cathy.

"Sure, the store has an alarm system but not the storage room because it was originally built to hold only janitorial supplies, not valuables and no employee except for the store manager and the pharmacist have a key. They're both family members so only they know what's stored in the room."

By now this tale is starting to grow legs, so I decide to dive into the dialogue. "Okay, Bones, your inside source knows something that nobody outside the family is supposed to know, is that right?"

"Right, and the only reason he knows is because he was once an assistant manager in training until he got fired."

"What he do, tap a till?" said Wilma laughing all by herself.

"No, he got arrested for residential burglary. Apparently he had a dope habit that was a little out of control and one day two detectives came and arrested him right from the store's sales floor."

"So where's he at now?" I ask.

"He's dead."

"DEAD!" we all echoed.

"Yeah, he was doing his time at Avenal State Prison when he caught Valley Fever."

"Gee, that sucks," said Cathy.

"So your source was his celly?"

"That, I'm not sayin', but you know how prisoners talk but only about a fraction of what comes out of their mouths is true, right?"

"RIGHT", we all echo now that Bones has us sucked in.

"So based on what My Lai has said, you believe this thing has legs?"

"I'm ready to stake my life's savings on it, if I had one," said Bones grinning like a greedy hyena.

"Well, what do you need us for?" I ask. "I can't imagine pulling up in a U-Haul and loading canisters of diamonds onto the back of a truck."

"Right you are, Roxxy, and I'm not asking you to do any of that. All I need is the three of you to figure a way into the storage room and make sure the merchandise is there and not a fake."

"Okay, so when we figure a way in how do we test it.?"

"I got you covered," said Bones. "The simplest test for diamonds besides cutting glass is they won't dissolve in acid. I'll supply the acid kits. All you've got to do is run the tests and determine which containers are the real deal then retrieve us a sample that I can take back to the financers of this heist."

"What are you gonna do with the synthetic gems?"

"We're not going to waste time with that, just identify the diamond canisters. I suspect there's a color code schematic, so make a mental note of that too."

"What's our take for this risk?" sighed Cathy.

"Three million cash, that's after the diamonds are sold."

"Ha, you mean we don't have to rip them off nor sell them?" piped Wilma whom all of us thought had passed out from drinking so much.

"No, because if we did, we probably wouldn't live long enough to spend any of it."

"Oh, so your financiers are like that?" spouted Cathy.

ROXXY

"Right, they play rough and they play for keeps."

* * *

CHAPTER FOUR

Bobbie Ray

Saturday
Strawberry Canyon
Berkeley, California

MY LITTLE HOMECOMING party was unusually good. Bones'
monster heist was interesting, but it left me feeling a little uneasy. It
wasn't like him to take on a job without getting a chunk of money in
advance. Cathy and I sensed there was something he wasn't telling us.
Perhaps he was in over his head with whoever we were supposed to be
working for, some hooligans he couldn't tell us anything about.

I trusted Bones but only to a point. I knew he was depending on me.
I decided to go along with his caper and see how it would turn out. My
job was supposed to be easy, and how I wanted to work it was left up
to me, although I knew I'd have to allow My Lai to prove her worth
before I'd let her become a part of our clan. I told Bones I needed at
least a couple weeks to work everything out. He was too anxious for my
style. He had no choice. It was my way or he could do it himself.
Besides, Miss. Kenny had invited me to his homecoming party. I
expected there'd be some drama and adventure, an event I dare not miss.

ROXXY

The poolside garden party was up in the Berkeley Hills, at this castle like residence near Strawberry Canyon. It was Miss. Kenny's get out of jail homecoming. He'd only done four months, but to young Kenny's spoiled ass it must-of seemed like a century.

My date, of course, was Esquire Cash. Karrene was a Cal Berkeley grad. She introduced me to few of her sorority club sista's. I expected them to be cavalier and uppity but they weren't. I decided to create my own fun with them so I slipped into a silly role play. I used a fake French African accent and dropped my natural tone an octave or two.

"I am from Guyana, please to meet chew," or, "I am here on student visa. I study at Stan-ford Uni-vercity." I showed a lot of teeth and bugged my eyes and it worked. Karrene didn't mess with my mischievousness. She thought it was hilarious. She was an adventure seeker, same as me. Besides, the party needed a little "Bang!" Eventually, I got swamped with a zillion questions by one of Karrene's lesbian friends. She was trying to hit on me, so I went to plan 'B', faked a sore throat and made a dash for the poolside bar.

The poolside party was an elaborate backyard garden set, with flowering hibiscus, gladiolus, and azalea plants. The kidney shaped pool was steamy and aqua blue. There were several Grecian styled urns bordering it and two clay lion heads were spouting water on opposite sides. White and goldenrod Japanese lanterns outlined a cobblestone deck and a pathway led to a spacious marble platform where a ten-piece band was playing some old school Chris Botti and Michael Buble swank. Most of the women wore floral print dresses and open-toe platform styled heels. The men wore white and powder-blue dinner jackets, with matching bow-ties and monogrammed cufflinks on starched white shirts.

After getting myself a cocktail, I hung out at the buffet that was set up next to the bar. I nibbled on shish kebab and sipped on a Mohido, some type of exotic mix. I was tapping my toes to this jazzy instrumental, a tune I'd heard before, and suddenly the lyrics were on the tip of my tongue...

"...Some-where...beyond the sea...my love's waiting for me...I'd like to fly like a bird up hi—eye...just beyond the sea, when I go, sail—lyn..."

Wow, I was feelin' it when this broad shouldered six-foot-three Adonis with jet black ringlets of curly hair was smiling at me. He was draped in a white silk open-collar shirt, tapered cobalt blue trousers, and a pair of white oxfords. His hands were big and so were his feet. He was loud.

"You can close your mouth, pretty mama," he said with a raspy chuckle. He obviously got off on seeing me look stupid. I couldn't answer right away. I continued to chew and gaze at him like I was looking up at the Leaning Tower of Pizza, bronze skin, thick brush mustache, narrow hips and no ass at all. I knew men built like that often had long slim dicks. It doesn't take a woman but a few seconds to know whether she wants a guy to seduce her. My insides were screaming for him. If given the chance, I'd let him fuck me like an android. I wasn't one to cream on myself but I imagined he was licking my clit like a salamander. He looked to be about fortyish, a young OG with a chiseled body and ocher brown predator eyes. To put it simple, the nigga' was "fine". Anyway, when he told me to close my mouth, "Huh?" was about all I could utter. I was in a tailspin.

He stepped forward, "My-my, you got some pretty lips, girl," he teased. "I would certainly row 'de boat for you, surgah'!"

There was no shyness in his nonsense for short limericks. I took a Mohido and smiled, "I bet you would," I replied. "Don't tell me, you're a sailor who just happened to dock port-side and the band is playing your song."

This time he didn't smile but tilted his gorgeous head to listen, "Oh that...that's a Bobby Darin imitation."

"Well, it's pretty."

"Yeah, like I was just saying, so are your lips."

I allowed myself to blush this time.

"My name's Bobbie Ray Cash. My friends call me, Ray. You mind if I call you Beautiful? "

"Sure, go right ahead, Ray."

I'm wearing a satin turquoise evening gown with a cowl neckline, complete with gold accessories; necklace, charm bracelets, jeweled belt, and three-inch Spartan heels. I'm showing off a lot of thigh. The brocaded gown is slit from the hips down.

He scoots a barstool up close to me, reaches inside his trouser pocket and offers me a cigarette. I refuse because I have my own. I remove one from my clutch purse and he lights it for me. I take a pull from mine and release a stream of smoke. Our eyes are locked like heat sinking missiles, "My name's Roxanne. My friends call me, Roxxy," I say borrowing Marylyn Monroe's sexier voice just for a minute, and throwing his spiel right back at him. "So, you're one of Karrene's brothers?" I lean into his shoulder before he can answer and I point at his match book. He gave me a puzzled look and hands it over. I read the words, 'Casa Blanca Room'. "Is that a gambling joint or a hotel?"

"Actually it's a little of both."

"Is that where you're staying?"

"Only when I have company."

I smile, "Company?"

"Yeah, with a pretty woman like you."

He wasn't the smoothest talker I ever met but I liked his persistence. Besides, I'd already made up my mind. My libido was up, and like I said before, I needed a good fuck. So we left the poolside garden party just as the guest of honor, Miss. Kenny, arrived. Karrene had already peeped us and was preoccupied being presidential with her sorority chicks. So I sent her a text to say 'thanks, goodbye, and I'm leaving with your brother'.

* * *

Bobbie Ray's ride was a vintage 2002 convertible Rolls Corniche, white with tan leather interior.

"Ooou, I like this bucket, Ray!" I was being mischievous, rubbing my palms over the leathered dash and seats as though I wasn't use to being in luxury. I think Ray knew better, but just went along with the tease. I leaned on the console and snuggled up close so my strawberry curls could cascade across his shoulder. As soon as he flicked the ignition a silky instrumental came flowing from his unit.

"Is that Santana?"

He laughs, "No, it's Spyro Gyra. You like it?"

"Of course, but the balance is not quite right. You mind?" I didn't wait for an answer. I began my little tweak on a series of buttons. After having no success, Ray brushes my hand away.

"Stop right there. That's perfect. Relax yourself, silly girl. There's a bar in the back. Scoot your legs up."

I pull my knees to my breast as Ray flicks another switch and the passenger seat begins to slowly revolve. I'm now facing the mini-bar. I pretend I'm not impressed and immediately begin searching for a label of booze that's familiar to me. I grab a bottle of Courvoisier. I take a swill and pass him the bottle.

"Roxxy, pour some in one of those cups," he says as he pulls the car out of the parking lot and into the street.

I follow his lead but overfill his cup and some spills on his slacks.

"Damn," he chuckles, "that booze is cold."

Before he can finish toweling himself off, I flick the switch and return the passenger seat back to its normal position. "Let me have a look," I said while copping a feel. Ray watches my other hand disappear between the zipper of his fly as I find the slit in his boxers and begin massaging his dick. I love giving an unsuspecting man a hard-on. Half of the fun is watching the shriveled thing stretch.

"Damn, surgah', let me pull over, girl!"

But he didn't.

"Humph, you real good at that, ain't cha'?" he surrendered.

I was loving it. I'm giggling inside because there's nothing he can do about it except take it. "Like you told me a minute ago, Ray, relax yourself, honey." Then suddenly, Bobbie Ray pulls over and parks, which stops me from doing what I do best. He pushes my hand away. Now I'm pissed.

"What's wrong with you, Ray? I know you're not about to tell me you're gay!

Ray chuckles, he's holding on to my bony wrist and his cucumber is saluting me. Then he gave me that disarming grin of his.

"I got a rough past, Roxxy"

"Well, I'm a matured woman, in case you didn't know. What are you, a serial killer?"

"No, kinky woman, I'm married."

"Ha, tell me somethin' I haven't already figured, Ray."

"She's my third and she's my business partner."

"So," I say.

"I just wanted you to know."

"Look, pretty, nigga'," I grab his dick and press my tits against his chest. Our eyes weld and we kiss...a phat long juicy one. His sausage fingers travel between my legs and he slips two of them into my slit. He grunts and I moan because I'm already wet. My five senses are working overtime. I'm certain he can smell my Chanel No. 5 and I'm smelling his cigarette breath. I wasn't certain how or when he freed his hand from my vagina's crevice and replaced it with his slim-jim. Umph...the nigga's dick had texture. My pussy lips have never lied. "Ooou-wee!" There's nothing like having sex in an expensive car. The windows steamed up in a matter of seconds. As Ray reclined the driver's seat, I pressed my palms against his chest and rode him like a dope fiend performing for a hit. Ray allowed me to have it my way but only to a point. He squeezed my buttocks to control my gyrations. He was messin' with my flow, so I pulled him out and gave his python a squeeze...I guess it was too much too soon...He gasped, then exploded...and globes of cum webbed my hair, neck and face.

* * *

Me and Bobbie Ray finally did find our way to the Casa Blanca Room but we made a stop at the bar and got stuck. I had a real good time. We got smashed, so we had Karrene and one of her girlfriends come to our rescue and drive us home.

I got up the next day around six. Mugsy and I took a Sunday drive. The downtown streets of San Jose looked deserted. It felt rather nice. The weather girl said it was going to be an unusually warm April day, somewhere in the 80's she predicted. I drove to the Burbank section, Rose Garden Park. I let Mugsy roam and then Cathy called.

"Hey Roxanne, I was hoping you were up."

"Girl, you must know that Mugsy is not gonna let me sleep in. He'll pull my bed covers off just to make sure I feed his fat ass. So why are you up so early?"

"My car is at my mechanic's house, and My Lai is on her way to get me so I can pick it up. Then afterwards, we're having breakfast in the Pruneyard."

"At that Omelet House, I bet?"

"Un-huh, why don't you join us?"

"That I can do. But you must know the doors don't open for business until around eight-thirty."

"I know, but there's going to be a line of people, so it's best we get there early."

"What about me calling Wilma?"

"I already did that. She's asleep. I left her a message on voice mail. I'll give her a call-back later."

Mugsy and I pulled up at The Pruneyard around eight o'clock. The Omelet's patron line was already forty people deep, but there was no sign of Cathy or My Lai. I parked for fifteen minutes and decided to take a place in line. When the girls finally showed up, Wilma was with them. Cathy was driving her '55" Cadillac, rag-top convertible, a .331d V8, dual four-barrel carburetor, power everything, steering, brakes, windows and seats. The leather interior was carmine red, radial tires with Sabre spoked wheels. The hoopty was clean. Cathy had the stereo turned up loud enough to wake up everyone living within a two block radius. The girls piled out of the car like they was drunk, laughing and loud talkin'. I held my place in line until they finally spotted me and paraded on over.

"What's going on with ya'll?"

"Girl, you should have been with us, Roxanne. You missed the Boo-ya!" proclaims Wilma.

"The Boo-ya?"

Cathy's rolling her eyes, which is her way of saying that Wilma's exaggerating, and My Lai has got this smug look on her face like she's just cut up her lover's wardrobe and burned it. By now, my anticipation for a straight answer has gotten the best of me.

"Oh-kay, so I'm clueless."

"We just blew up a car," boasted Wilma.

"You did what!" I say trying to whisper, not wanting just anybody to hear our conversation.

"My Lai made a cocktail and dropped it in her boyfriend's gas tank."

"A cocktail?"

"He not pay. An' he owed me a lot of money," blurts My Lai shrugging her shoulders, then flicking the ash from her cigarette before sticking it back in the left corner of her mouth.

"This girl is the real deal," said Cathy. "You know how hard it is to impress me and I'm impressed. She pinched a tiny hole in a ping-pong ball and filled it with Drain-O. Then she dropped it in. We had to wait about ten minutes before it blew up."

"So, nobody was hurt?"

"Hell-no!" answered Wilma. "But her boyfriend came running out the house wearing nothing but a bath towel and he was cursing in seven different languages."

I look back at My Lai and now she's smiling. She's got a mouth like a Muppet, wide open but no lips.

"I say, payback is a motha'," said My Lai. "I just send him a message. He'll pay me now."

I gave her my palm and she removed the cigarette from the corner of her mouth, and slapped my outstretched hand. I'm diggin' this chick. She's a skinny little shit but she's got a set of balls.

Twenty minutes later, the restaurant opens and it took another ten minutes before we were seated inside. Their specialty was omelets of course and everything they served was huge, huge plates, huge side orders, and huge glasses of juice and milk. We could have ordered two plates and had enough to feed six people. Nothing went to waste. Mugsy was waiting in my Lexus and about to go zonkers over this huge doggie bag.

After we were done eating we couldn't smoke inside, so we paid the tab, left a fat tip, then had our smoke in the courtyard of the plaza.

"Check-it-out, girls, let's get serious for a minute. We got this job to look forward to, but first, we've got to get hold of the key to that storeroom."

I reach inside my Gucci bag and removed a folded sheet of paper. It's a sketch.

"Now, what you're looking at is the drug store layout. It's huge, about twelve thousand square feet, a dozen isles, an ice cream counter near the front entrance and six check-out stands. To the far west corner, is 'Isle number one': toiletries, cosmetics, cameras, and miscellaneous stuff. On the northwest wall, Isle ten, small appliances, auto and household accessories. Just a couple yards east is the building's rear exit loading dock and warehouse area. And next to that is the pharmacy and manager's office. It's elevated by a short flight of stairs, seven steps. To the right, is the hallway which leads to a break room and the cold storage of beverages is actually on the corner, right here," I indicate by pointing a finger. "Now, directly behind it is our target, the smaller storage room with containers of diamonds, gold and other gems. Tomorrow morning, we can go in as shoppers. Dress anyway you want but we don't go in together. Wilma and Cathy, you two go in first. At 10:00 o'clock sharp, you two start a commotion at the camera section right about here," I point and look them in the eye. "Nothing overly dramatic but make it loud, and make sure it lasts a good ten minutes.

My Lai, you're gonna be posted up over here," again I point, "with a shopping basket in your arm—"

"Oh what time do I come inside the store?" interrupted My Lai.

"You and I are coming in five minutes behind Cathy and Wilma. You lead and I'll trail. Now, while I'm haggling with the pharmacist, I'll coax him to come down from his booth and when I do, you be ready to zip up the stairs and make an impression of this key." I hand her a picture. It's a blowup.

My Lai frowns, "One key?"

"Yes. There will be a set of keys on a rig on this wall," I reach inside my purse and pull another sketch. "This is the office layout."

"Ahh, Miss. Roxanne."

"Call me Roxxy, surga', what is it?"

"It's better if I wear a druggist coat or a clerk's smock. I can carry one in a bag and duck into, here."

She points at the wide rear exit area that leads to the warehouse section.

"Okay, I see what you mean. Improvise anyway you want, but once you leave that office make sure you have the right key impression and if there's a problem, don't panic. I'll have your back. You know we're planning this but anything can happen, and things could go wrong."

I return my attention to Cathy and Wilma, "You two know how to work your magic. Monday morning is phase-one. Phase-two, My Lai will take the key impression and have the key made for pick-up no later than Wednesday morning."

"Wednesday?"

"Yeah, because that's the day I'm going in as a shopper, and that's when I will make sure the key fits. Cathy, you'll watch my back."

"What about cameras?" asked Wilma.

"We're not gonna worry about cameras. Just make sure that every time you enter the store you bring a different look, wigs, shades, whatever, because at some point after this caper is pulled off, some security expert is going to be looking over a lot of film."

"So what day do we go in and identify the merchandise?" inquires Wilma. Her eyes are looming like big exclamation points.

"I won't have an answer for that until I talk to Bones, but just for right now, what we've discussed stays with us four. Leave Bones to me...I'd like to keep him in suspense."

* * *

Monday's Thrift Drug Store run came off pretty much like we planned. Everyone getting into character was the easy part. By 9:45 a.m. the store was buzzing with activity. Most of the isles were flooded with boxes of stockroom cargo as venders and employees were busy setting up displays and restocking shelves, and early bird shoppers were on the hunt for bargains.

At 10:15 sharp, there was a loud crash on isle number one. Someone tipped an eyeglass and sunshade display which upended a hosiery display that fell on a woman who was browsing over a greeting card display. An argument between three female patrons became a loud calamity as My Lai and I began synchronizing our moves.

The pharmacist was easy, past middle-aged and balding. Once he zeroed in on my loose fitting low-cut halter, his bulbous eyes were fastened to my bra-less jiggling jugs. While he insisted on helping me find a product that didn't exist, I got close enough to allow him to cop an incidental feel.

"Oh, excuse me, my bad," I said as I leaned a little more and pressed my tit against his shoulder. I was wearing skin tight acrylics that displayed every dimple in my ass, so the pervert was trying to grope and I let him.

My Lai was agile and quick. She must have jetted up the stairway because I didn't see her go in but I spotted her coming out. She was wearing a gold smock with a 'Thrifty' name tag on it. Later the four of us reconvened in the shopping center's parking lot where we laughed and bragged about nothing but fun. My Lai complained that all the keys looked alike, so she took three impressions. I didn't see a problem with that unless she'd gotten them all wrong. I hoped not, but I'd find out soon enough.

Wednesday arrived with a muggy overcast-sky and a threat of rain. Cathy and I wore see-thru raincoats. I got all dolled up and wore my Spartan heels and a micro-mini. The beverage cooler was on the right of a short hallway, and a fifteen-foot wall of office glass was to the left, which gave the store's manager and pharmacist a clear view of almost everyone below. I didn't know where the manager was but I could clearly see that the pharmacist was preoccupied. The storage room was the second room right passed a water cooler. Customer foot traffic was light as I made my move.

The first two key's I tried didn't work, so I said a quick, silent prayer and the third key slipped right in. Cathy and I used cell phones to communicate. My plan was to spend no more than five minutes in. At first, I couldn't find a light switch so I used a Bic lighter to roam in the dark. The room wasn't big. There were two small desks, one by the door and one on the opposite wall. Suddenly, I bumped it and tipped over a lamp. I rescued the lamp and flicked it on. Even after removing its shade the forty-watt bulb was a poor excuse for light. I held the lamp high above my head and just began to get a decent look around when my cell phone chirped...

"Roxanne!! It's the pharmacist!! He's already at the door and he's fiddling with his key ring."

"Okay, hold your position, Cat, and stay on line, cuz I got this."

I immediately removed my raincoat, turned off the lamp, and struck a pose by sitting on top of the desk and crossing my legs. The pharmacist came jittering and fumbling through the doorway like a man who had just entered a bathroom and was anxious to take a tinkle. Suddenly, he flipped a switch and a blue overhead light shadowed the tiny room. Then the pharmacist removed a porn magazine from his rear pocket, loosened his belt, and his trousers dropped to the floor. Just as he was putting a serious squeeze on his noodle--he must of caught a glimpse of me from the corner of his eye--It took every ounce of control to keep me from laughing because the man must of leaped about five feet off the floor! But the comedy ended when he got tangled in his pants and thumped his forehead against the desk and tumbled to the floor. Instantly, there was oozing blood.

"My pah-pit-pills," he stuttered.

I rushed to his side and searched frantically through his pockets. Then I screeched into my cell, "Call the paramedics!"

"Hurry up, cuz he's turning blue!"

I managed to rescue some pills from his coat pocket and tried to give him one. I got it down his throat but his breathing had already stopped. I placed my ear to his chest and prayed for a pulse... I think the man was dead. His eyes had already closed.

*   *   *

CHAPTER FIVE

Kill Chip

ME AND CATHY WILSON bolted from the parking lot just as the paramedics arrived. We saved our conversation until we were cruising along a stretch of San Thomas Expressway.

"Well, did you kill 'em?"

"No! I didn't kill 'em, Cat. The man had a sweaty plump face. He looked slimy like he was having a stroke or something. I found his heart pills and gave him one before he tapped out."

"I can see it now, Headline news, Roxanne, film at eleven!"

"I doubt it."

"Why?"

"Because nobody saw me go in and nobody saw me come out."

"Are you sure?"

"Trust me, Cat. Even if I'm on camera," I took off my black wig and removed my sunglasses, "how can a camera identify me?"

"Humph, you ever heard of face-print technology?"

"What do you take me for, a Kronut? Of course I've heard about it. The government has got it but they can't use or enforce it without consent."

"Okay, Tru-dat. What about virtual autopsy?"

"No, but I guess you're gonna tell me."

Cathy pushes inward on the dashboard cigarette lighter, and taps a filtered cigarette on her steering wheel before sticking it in her mouth.

She smokes Marlboros and I hate them cuz they stink. The expressway traffic has slowed, it's high noon, the rain has stopped, and the weather is starting to heat up.

"Check this out, home girl. Virtual autopsy is a computer generated crime scene program. It's a 3D scan with an infrared laser. It will virtually take a picture of everything in a room, blood splatter, point of impact——"

"Kill the momma drama, Cat! You're scaring me and I don't like it. First of all, I didn't murder nobody. The man's death, if he's dead, was an accident."

"Yeah, you and I know that but all it takes is some jive-ass inspector Clue-so to stumble on something, then you and I are toast."

Cathy wasn't listening, so I put on one of her quiet CD's, a Shubert sonata in 'A' minor, a little somethin' to help calm her but she wouldn't shut up.

"Like I was sayin', girl, all I need is one of them private dicks puttin' out a bolo search for my Cadillac..."

Traffic was at a snail's pace and I'd had enough, "Pull over, Cat and let me out, cuz you're making me sick!"

Cathy looked back at me with no make-up on her face and gave me those sad Oprah Winfrey eyes again, "You're right, Roxanne, my bad. But now what?"

"What do you mean, 'now what'?"

"What do we tell Bones?"

"We don't tell nobody nothing that they don't need to know. Except this," I said in a whisper as though I didn't want my own conscience to record what I was about to say. "We let Bones and the girls know the storage room was spotless, and there were no diamonds or gold in there. Besides, I knew something was cauliflower about this caper. If I was a man I'd fuck Bones up just for getting' me involved in this mess."

"Humph, me too! But I sure would have liked to have gotten my hands on some of them chocolate diamonds. Them babies is the shit!"

"Well, let's get real, Cat, it didn't make any real sense to be holding that much cheddar in any room except an office with a walled-in safe."

"Ooou, Roxanne, we got Jedi-like minds, girl, cuz I was thinking the same thing."

* * *

Cathy dropped me off at my place and my day went back to normal. After giving Mugsy a bath, I stopped by the rehab drop-in clinic. The counselor was busy, and I was still feeling a little uneasy. Cathy was probably right, I had caused the Pharmacist's death. So I eased that nagging thought aside. I took a seat in the lobby and gave Bones a call. Bones was disappointed and in disbelief. He said he was counting on this caper to help him tie up some loose ends. Bones owned a twin-engine airplane and had recently purchased a Riva Domino, a sleek and speedy Italian made yacht. The plane's warehousing and pilot fees were costing more than a pretty penny, but I betcha that wasn't his real problem. Bones was a chronic gambler. He'd bet on everything, football, basketball, horse racing, and NASCAR. He's even bet on rodeo bronco riding to see if the rider would reach the qualifying eight seconds or not. But I really wasn't worried about him. I was more concerned about his circle of hoodlum friends. Since I had stuck my neck out for him, I wasn't ready to drop everything and blow this caper off. Besides, I had to pay him back his ten G's.

After a bullshit conference with my counselor, I left the clinic and headed for My Lai's place of employment, the Brinks armored car garage, and waited for her to clock out.

My Lai was smart. Besides having a third eye in her forebrain, she had a fourth behind her neck. Before boarding her Jeep Cherokee, she spotted my Lexus and pulled up beside me.

"Let's roll," she said. She gave me a wave and led the way. I don't know where she was going but she wanted me to follow. When we turned into an apartment complex that sat directly across from the Thrifty Drug Shopping Center, the same uneasy feeling crept over me again. Apparently My Lai Smith owned a condo, a place she recently bought with cold cash under the name Sarah Lee. The home had all the modern amenities, brick fireplace, a terrace, range, refrigerator, washer and dryer. The freshly painted walls and new carpet gave it a nice aroma, but it was empty of any real furniture. It sounded hallow as we walked and our voices echoed when we talked.

This is my little hideaway," she said. "Nobody knows I own this place except you," she teased. "You want a drink?"

"Sure, what are we having?"

"Vodka and fruit juice."

I make a funny face.

"Oh, it's chilled, honey. Trust me, you'll like it."

I trailed her to the kitchen and gave her the latest news and she laughed through my entire explanation. It was kind of funny but not that funny.

"Are you sure the pharmacist is even dead? I know for a fact that sometimes people pass out during a stroke or heart attack for several minutes but they are often revived."

"Revived?" I was hoping she was right but still not convinced. She continued talking.

"Yeah, that pharmacist probably isn't dead. I bet he's laid up in some hospital room until he gets better."

The vodka and fruit juice seemed to clear the fog in my brain, and what My Lai was saying made perfect sense, so I made a call.

"May I speak to Nurse Joy?"

A voice said, "Yes, please hold."

As I waited, My Lai lit a blunt and passed it over to me.

"Hello."

"Nurse Joy, this is Roxanne Blackwell. Remember me?"

"Oh-yes, Miss. Blackwell, how are you?"

"I'm fine, surga'. Listen, I have a friend who may have checked into your hospital today a little before noon. His name is Mr. Patel. Can you tell me what room he's in? I'd like to come and see him."

"Hold on Miss. Blackwell, let me check for you."

Seconds later, "I have a Mr. George Patel who checked into emergency this morning but checked out this afternoon."

"Are you sure?"

"Yes, he had a mild stroke according to the index. Mild strokes are seldom serious enough to keep a patient overnight."

"Well, that's great news, thanks."

As I ended the call, My Lai was grinning like a Muppet again.

"I told you so!"

"Okay, so you did, Miss. Me Lie-Sarah Lee. You obviously know more than you're telling, so what's your secret and are we on the same team?"

"Of course we are but first you should tell me one of your secrets and I'll tell you one of mine."

"What do you want to know?"

"They say you're a Call-Girl, but I never see your pimp, so you must be very lucky or very smart."

"Oh, so you wanna get into the business, is that it?"

My Lai looks back at me with squinty eyes and takes another hit off the blunt, "No, but tell me why you work for Bones?"

"I don't work for Bones. I work with him on occasion. I don't need Bones He needs me."

"You mean he uses you just like he's trying to use me."

"Oh, really?"

"Yes really. How much you know about Bones past?"

"Not much, but I got this sneaky suspicion you're gonna tell me."

My Lai takes a sip of vodka and juice and cracks the knuckles in her left hand. I brace myself just in case she decides to throw a punch.

"Bones and my father, Jessie Smith, were in the military together. My father was an army captain and Bones was a transport and warehouse sergeant. Bones ran the books. He was deep into the Black Marker business and was able to make a cargo plane disappear on paper. When they discharged, Bones got a job running the shipping and receiving warehouse of a department store chain. Later, he got my father hired as an executive head in the accounting department. My father didn't need the job. He had a military pension and had sunk the majority of his savings into the real estate market. My father knew Bones was always running some type of scheme, but he didn't know how deep he was in until it was too late. From day one, even before my father was hired, Bones was fleecing the company and cooking the books by making cargos of merchandise disappear. At first he pretended to keep my father safe and out of the loop, but when the shit hit the fan and his scheme was exposed, Jessie Smith's name appeared on several of the major transactions. It was forgery but my father's lawyer failed to prove it. Both Bones and my father went down for the beef. They were charged with conspiracy to commit fraud and embezzlement of thirty million dollars. Bones made a deal that placed the crux of the crimes on my father. Bones got six years and my father got fifteen. The courts took my father's real estate holdings as payment in restitution and it broke him. After his ninth year in prison cancer showed up in his prostate and he died last year."

"Whoa, My Lai, I'm sorry to hear—"

"Hey, that's life. Shit happens. Bones knows Captain Jessie Smith has died, but what he doesn't know is that I'm his daughter."

"So, what are you planning to do about it.?"

"Roxanne, revenge is a motha' fuck, and I'm here to flip game on Bones just like he flipped on my father."

This is a lot of new info on Bag of Bones-Bones and it's very intriguing, but I'm not surprised. Maybe I'm just fortunate he hasn't had reason to burn me.

"Okay," I say, "so let's talk diamonds."

My Lai relights the blunt and tries to pass it over to me. I throw a palm up, because I've had enough. After hearing her dad's story, I'm feeling a little angry and I don't know exactly why.

"The Thrifty Drug diamonds is not a bunch of hype," said My Lai. There is a stash but Bones only knows part of the real story. I did some research and I think I know the rest."

"But didn't Bones get his info from the backers that are financing the heist?"

"Ha! Bones got the gift of gab, but he shooting us a line of bull. He ain't got no backers but his greedy self. He just tossed up that three-million-dollar figure to entice you to do his grunt work."

"So tell me something I don't know?" I said.

My Lai stands up and motions at me to follow her into the living room. We end up looking out the front room's picture window in silence. Once again the queasy feeling comes over me as I scan the buildings that make up the Drug Thrift Store shopping mall. There's a fabric store and next to it is a women's shoe store, a small screen cinema, a food mart, and a Country Western bar. Examining the buildings was like actually seeing them for the first time.

"What I didn't explain on the night of your homecoming," said My Lai, "was the Patel's own the entire strip mall. Not just the Drug Thrift Store. You see that fabric shop next to it?"

"Yeah, what about it?"

"I made a trip to the county records library and researched the strip mall's architectural layouts. There's an underground walkway that connects the two buildings."

"You're kidding!"

"No, I'm not. Did you get a good look around when you were inside that storage room?"

"I didn't have time. The lighting was poor and the pervert pharmacist didn't give me a chance."

"Well, my guess is that those canisters of diamonds that Bones was talking about are being kept in the basement of the fabric store, and the Thrifty Drug Store's storeroom may be the only way to access it."

"Okay, so if this is true then we both know the way in but how do we get them out?"

"I've got an idea but it will take some planning. Do you shoot?"
"Shoot?"

My Lai reaches around her back and from underneath her jacket she comes out with a 9 millimeter Glock 17, equipped with a sixteen round clip.

"Oh-that!" I say, feeling a little stunned. "I'm not really into guns, but I ain't scared to shoot a monk if I have to." I showed her a nickel plated .25 Raven automatic with six in the clip and one in the chamber. It was a little something I had stashed inside my Louis Vuitton.

* * *

I have no way of really knowing if My Lai is bullshitting me or not. She certainly tells a compelling story. I like her spirit, but a small voice inside said I should invest some time into checking her out.

The next day, I had a full list of things to do, but first I had a yearning for some new clothes. After giving Mugsy his morning run, I drove to Palo Alto's Stanford Shopping Mall. When I pulled into a parking stall, I thought I recognized a familiar face. A petite female was leaning against a silver Lincoln Suburban. She was decked out in candy apple red leggings, short spike heeled boots, a white leather waist jacket, and a black pleated mini. Her frizzy wig was bushy and pink, and she was smoking what seemed like a foot-long cigarette with an inch of ash that refused to fall. I took a closer glance as I passed her by and I realized it was Miss. Kenny.

"Hello Elmo," I said. I had just taken a couple nips from a flask of Courvoisier, so I was a little tipsy myself.

"Excuse me. My name is not Elmo, Miss. whoever you supposed to be. An' why are you up in my biz-ness? You need to just beat-it!"

Kenny did his malicious bitch imitation better than most project chicks I know. He was waving his hands and posturing like he had a big booty the same size as Nicki Minaj.

"Kenny! Don't you recognize me? What are you doing here?"

Kenny is peeking over the rim of his Versace designer sunglasses, "Roxanne, is that really you? What did you do, change your hair? You look so different from the first time I met you."

"Well, look who's talking. What's going on, and why are you all frocked up in costume, cuz I thought you told me you weren't into that sort of thing."

"I'm here with my man, silly. An' this is the way he wants me to look. We're getting ready to go shopping."

I take a look around, "Well, where is he hiding at?" I tease.

"He's over on the next row of cars helping some old lady get her hoopty started. Oh, look here he comes now!"

I turn to see this big bastard, about six-foot somethin'. He's swinging a MiniTool box in his right hand, and he's wearing a blue billed sea captain's hat that was a least two sizes smaller than his head. He wore a faded Hawaiian shirt that fit him like a moo-moo, white cargo shorts, and a pair of deck shoes covered in oil stains. Miss. Kenny doesn't give him a chance to reach us. He prances over to him like he's Pepe la Pew's girlfriend as he grabs the man's bear paw. With his free hand, the giant tucks little Kenny under his armpit and squeezes the boy's butt. I'm six-one in heels and this man is actually hovering over me like a tree. He's looking me over with demon eyes, ocher brown irises with a yellowish tint.

"Roxanne, this is Houston," said Kenny in a sing-song voice. Miss. Kenny is puckering his Kool-Aid lips and squints his heavily mascara eyes like he's just stepped out of a Botox clinic. I nod once and smile. Houston tips his sailor's cap as Kenny's midget hand disappears between his sugar daddy's tree trunks for thighs. I'm thinking this nigga' must have a donkey dick, because his deck shoes are huge!

"Oh, so you're Karrene's brother," I manage to say as I snap the awkward moment of silence.

Once again, Houston nods, "Yes, I am." But he's looking at me like he either wishes I hadn't known that or he just wants me to go away.

"Excuse me," I say, "but I'm on a tight schedule so I've gotta run, nice to have met you, Houston." I bend forward and peck Kenny on the cheek and he whispered in my ear.

"You need to give Bobbie Ray a holler." And for a millisecond, hearing the name made my left nipple twitch.

* * *

I tried shopping at Nordstrom's but couldn't find anything I liked, so I exited to the potty room and sent a text to Ray. I was pampering myself when he texted me back, he'd reserved a suite at the Casa Blanca Room. He said the desk clerk had a key reserved for my use, and he'd be there around ten-ish. I was glad that Ray was still thinking about me, because I certainly hadn't forgotten about him. His timing was perfect since Miss. Rose would be paying me a visit in two more days and my pussy couldn't wait to get beat up. Besides, I had a gang of clients that I couldn't continue to neglect. I had four quickies scheduled from 2:00 to 7:00 p.m. They were my average three to five thousand dollar tricks. I did a fox-trot over to Victoria's Secret and picked a fresh black negligee with peek-a-boo breast flaps, a garter belt bottom, net stockings, and a pair of glass heeled stilettos. The merchandise was cheap and would get me through the night.

I met my two o'clock trick in a vacant office space up in San Jose's Santana Row, an extravagant shopping villa on the west side of town. My client was one of the vice-presidents of a Union Bank. He had a fetish for my cherry freckled areolas. For him, I really didn't need to perform or get undressed. I'd just drop my top and let him gobble up my goodies. He had to report back to his office by three, so I let him jerk some suds on my duds. It didn't take him but a minute to shoot a load of goo. He trembled with pleasure. It took ten minutes to cool him down. Once he regained his composure, he tossed me five g's and swooped out the door. My next stop was the Alameda Boulevard. I bought a ticket at a little theater where the marquee listed two French foreign films. This was a very old client of mine, a retired fire chief whose age might have been around seventy-five. He was waiting for me in the balcony's fifth row, seat number two-seventy-two. He was wearing his usual blue windbreaker with the word 'Windjammer' stenciled along each sleeve and a plaid pair of Bermuda shorts. We didn't talk. I took the seat next to him. He was holding onto a box of popcorn and continued to watch the movie house screen. Then he handed me the popcorn and I had to eat my way down to a wad of crisp hundred dollar bills. By the time I tucked the money in my bra, Pops had pulled up my skirt and was playing with his pee-pee. He slid his free hand between my legs and he let out a whimper as soon as his fingers touched my moist muffin. Earlier, I'd given myself an extra creamy douche to trick my customers into thinking they were making me wet. I licked his earlobe and watched his cum fly over the seat and into the next row. We were lucky nobody was sitting near us, cuz Pops was in a frenzy. I dashed from my seat and within seconds a theater usher with a flashlight arrived just as I zipped through a curtained exit. In the ladies' room I refreshed my make-up and checked my clothes for the sticky spunk.

It was only 4:00 p.m. and my next date was supposed to be set for five. I had about forty-five minutes to kill. There was a coffee shop next door so I ordered a latte and called my next client. I got a voice mail message that said he had to cancel. I guess our date wasn't meant to be. Then ten minutes later my fourth date texted me and Jack Dupont urged me to come early.

Jack was a trip. He was deep in chocolate chips, Franklin's and Jefferson's up the wahzoo. He was a thoroughbred trainer, who owned a horse ranch in the Almaden Hills. When I arrived at his western styled mansion, I was greeted by his butler and several stable hands. They always waved or whistled whenever I came by.

"Mr. Jack will be with you shortly, madam."

The butler was a middle aged man completely bald with a full red beard. He was always so polite in his pressed Levis stuffed in a pair of black riding boots. My wait in the parlor was a little longer than usual for someone who was asked to come early. Finally, this teenaged looking girl came down the spiral staircase to escort me up.

Jack was a bit of a jock, swimming, tennis, and of course horseback riding. He was a silver-haired O.G. with brown leathery sun beaten skin. By the time I entered his room, he had just finished smashing two other chicks, but it was apparent that neither could get him to cum. I really didn't know what he desired with all that pussy lying about. Jack was sprawled naked in the middle of a round double king sized bed. He had an aqua colored satin sheet covering one leg and his privates, but he must of shot up with something, because his skinny-ass dick had the sheet propped up like a tent.

How ya' doin' Miss. Cane?" Jack was talking loud like he was the director on some movie set, "Come in and join the party." He was showing me a big toothy grin. I get a foot within his reach and he yanks at my skirt, runs his hand up my thigh, and manages to grab a handful of ass. The man was rough and nasty. I almost lost my balance so I let him pull me into bed. He's fondling me like a monkey in heat. Then he tries to kiss me. He knows I don't play that but he tests me anyway. I slip my hand under the sheet and he grunts when I snatch his pole. I know how he likes it so he lets me do my thing.

I come out of my skirt and blouse and toss them aside. Underneath, is my black lingerie. Jack's hazel eyes widen because he likes what he sees. My tits are all swollen from my first clients manhandling. My cherry nipples are erect and I begin by rubbing them up and down his shaft. Then I give his balls a savage torque. He grunts and kicks for a sec but I don't let go. My plan is to save myself some work by jerking him into a frenzy.

"Hand me my Louis Vuitton," I said to the nearest girl.

"Huh?"

"My purse, honey."

I pulled out a miniature bottle of jasmine scented baby oil and my flask of Courvoisier. I chug some liquor and squirt my palms with oil and begin lathering up Jack's prick. For the first ten minutes I was having it my way until them two horny-ass bitches climbed back in bed. Jack's attention was diverted and his dick momentarily shriveled, so I had to suck it back to life. Less than five minutes passed and my jawbone started aching so I was about to give up, but just as I pulled my lips away to take a breath, Jack erupted. His slime-like, cum skeeted in three different directions, hitting me, the chicks, and himself. Globs of thick, syrupy spunk was spewing down the sides of his shaft like lava from a volcano. Jack must have had a month's worth of sperm juice up in him. He looked like he was in a state of shock. The brick red hood of his dick must have been sore from my sucks, cuz it was still twitching. I didn't get a chance to taste his spunk, because by the time I recovered, them greedy-ass bitches had gobbled him up.

Jack tipped me with seven G's and said he'd call me back in a couple of weeks. By the time I got on the road again, it was well past seven o'clock.

I liked the Casa Blanca Room. It had that nostalgic feel, like an old school gangsta' movie. It was a three storied building, shrouded in red and pink flowering camellias. Inside, there was lots of open space with a bar, dinning, gambling tables, and a counter for checking in. The furnishings were floral patterned carpets, Duncan Phyfe couches, cigar chairs and Tiffany lamps. The desk clerk was busy so I waited for just a bit.

"Did a Mr. Cash leave a message for---"

"Yes, he did Miss. Blackwell."

He handed me a key. It didn't take me long to figure out that the clerk remembered me from my prior visit. It's when Ray and I got stupid drunk.

I climbed two tiers of railed stairway. Ray's suite, which really wasn't a suite, was on the top floor. I found it not to be much bigger than a room at a Motel 6. It held a canopied bed, an antique dresser with a huge mirror, and a marble topped vanity equipped with a rack of towels. The bathroom was extra tiny, a toilet, a tub but no shower.

It was a warm spring night, so the first thing I did was slide open the drapes and the terrace's slim double glass doors. There was no TV, an old school radio and a black Ma Bell phone was on a bedside table. I tweaked the radio's dial until I found an easy listening station with smooth tunes. Then I made a call to the desk and had the Hop bring up a bottle of white wine. When the wine arrived, I tipped the Hop, and after a cool bath I got my nude body under a couple layers of cotton sheets and poured myself a glass of wine. By ten o'clock it didn't matter whether Bobbie Ray showed up or not, because I had planned to stay all night. After an hour of relaxing music and three glasses of wine, my eyelids told me it was time to let them close. I could feel a nice breeze coming through the terrace doors as I eased into a layer of sleep and finally drifting into a dream...

They came through my window, or through the slim terrace doors. Was it a dream——I wasn't sure, so rather than confront, I decided to lie still. A shadowy figure leaned over me, while another rummaged through a dresser drawer. I tossed and turned, my eyelids still closed, faking sleep. My .25 automatic was under my pillow—suddenly, a gloved hand slammed over my mouth, and I managed to bite a finger before a fist slugged me. My trigger finger flinched and a bullet whizzed past someone's head and shattered the dresser mirror. The fool who was straddling me wouldn't let go of my neck. I tried putting a knee to his groin and he chopped me in my ribs. The .25 was stripped from my hand and fell and even with my head dangling over the side, I still lost sight of the gun—then both men had me. One rifled through my purse-—I was clawing at my molester's face just as someone burst through the door...

IT WAS RAY!

Bobbie Ray wrestled the trick off me and gave him a whoppin'. I could hear grunts and thuds…then someone's elbow smashed the side of my head...

When I finally regained consciousness, Ray had a towel with ice over my left eye. The lights were on. The thugs were gone, and twenty dollar bills were scattered all over my bed. I guess I was lucky those Jackers were confused. Whatever they came to get they couldn't find it, and they didn't know what was more important, the money or my vagina. It's probably a good thing Ray showed up when he did, because if they would have took my pussy without payin', I would have had to pay someone to hunt them down. I must of told Ray "Thanks" about a hundred times but my ribs hurt so bad he had to take me to a hospital where I ended up staying overnight.

* * *

ROXXY

CHAPTER SIX

Bloodstones

IT WAS MORNING and the sunlight blinded my right eye as a familiar face loomed over me. It was Nurse Joy and she was smiling, but I must have been on some strong medication because as soon as I awakened, I faded out again...

Waking up in a chilly-ass hospital is no fun. My ribs are busted. My left eye is patched and swollen. Bobbie Ray saved my ass but he ain't sent no get well cards or a single bouquet. He act like his wifey got him pussy-whipped...Damn creep. I probably wouldn't be in this mess if it wasn't for him playin' with my feelings. I got better things to do Mista Cash. When my cell phone vibrated, I tried reaching for it, but my ribs hollered, "Stop!", so Nurse Joy was nearby and handed it to me.

It was Ray!

"Hello, Princess—"

"Princess-my-ass! You got me all twisted, Ray. I'm layin' here all jacked up and it's your fault. What was them hoodlums really looking for? Are you runnin' a store from that hotel?"

"A store?"

"Don't act like you dumb, nigga, cuz you know exactly what I mean!"

"Hold up, Roxxy. Don't go kamikaze on me, surgah. Yeah, I owe you an explanation, but we can't discuss this over the phone-—"

Our conversation is cut short and the call ends. I had heard a female's voice in the background before the phone hung up, and it's probably his wife. Then my cell phone goes off again.

"Who's this!" I bark.

"Is that any way to answer a client making a business call?"

"If you're in need of a date, then this isn't a good time, Bill."

"You don't say. Well, what's the matter, Candy it must be really serious if you're passing on earning some dough."

"It is serious. I had an accident and I may be laid up for a couple weeks."

"An accident? I'm sorry to hear that. You need me to do something for ya?"

"Not at the moment, but I'll give you a holler as soon as I get better." It was sweet that Nasty Bill made the offer, but as soon as I'd finished talking, Nurse Joy handed me a pair of crutches.

"What are these for?" I asked.

"I know you want to get out of here but you're going to need these."

At that instant I wanted to snatch the crutches from her outstretched hand, but I really didn't have the strength and I did need her help so I had to be nice.

Cathy Wilson had arranged for my Lexus to be towed from the Casa Blanca Room and returned to Terra Cotta Heights. Then she picked me up from the hospital a little before noon. The rib damage was on my left side, so I had to use at least one crutch to support myself. Cat helped me get situated in her Caddy's back seat, where I got as comfortable as I could. I searched through my purse and found my flask of booze. Once I took a swig I felt much better.

"What's new, Cat?"

"You are. So how did this happen?"

"You really don't wanna know. Let's just say I'm someone's collateral damage. Have you heard from Me Lie?"

"No, should I?"

"Un-huh, she and I are working on a little somethin', and she's gonna need your help since I'll be laid up for a while."

"Laid up? Are you planning on dying on me?"

"Don't worry, Cat, if I happen to die I'll still support you after I'm dead."

"How is that?"

"Because I'm gonna leave you some money, silly."

"Hot damn! Why don't you just go to sleep now so I can plant a kill-chip in ya."

"Ooou, you's a dirty bitch," I said to her as we both laughed loudly. "But seriously, Cat, My Lai may not need you, so just keep an eye on her anyway."

Before I could unlock the door to my penthouse, Mugsy was barking at me from the other side. Dogs have a way of knowing when something's gone wrong. Even though my neighbor had a key to look in on him, he must have picked up my scent. After humping my leg for about five minutes, Cathy took him out on a leash so he could handle his business. Next, I was running bath water when my cell phone screamed at me. The first was from Wilma. The next was from Bones. It was unusual for Wilma and Bones to call me back to back. They were acting all giddy like they were up to something. My gut told me they were screwing around somewhere outside of town. Then another client called and another. They were blowing up my phone. It went on like that for almost an hour. I got tired of explaining the same thing over and over, so I shut the damn thing off.

It took more than two weeks for my eye and ribs to heal, and just as I was about to step out for the evening, My Lai stopped over. She was carrying an economy sized box of Tampax. I'm amused by the goofy grin on her face. She sets the box on my living room coffee table. Then she skips over to my bar and pulls out a pint of liquor from inside her coat. It's a bottle of Smirnoff's whipped cream flavored vodka. She pours us each a glass.

"What are we celebrating?" I finally ask as we clink glasses.

"First, take a drink, have a seat, then open the box."

I quickly down my glass of Smirnoff and the taste is not bad. Then I snatch up the Tampax box. It's been opened then resealed with some type of Gorilla glue, so instead of fuckin' off my fresh designer nails, I get a bread-cutter from the kitchen and saw off the lid. My Lai is laughing at me but I don't care. I removed a pad and squeeze...nothing. I give My Lai a side-long glance. She winks and urges me to keep searching. The next pad I pick feels like it's got some gravel sealed inside. I rip it open and about a hundred gem stones came tumbling out, and I'm reaching and grabbing to keep them from bouncing off the table and under the couch. I must have looked real foolish, because My Lai is laughing so hard she spilled most of her drink.

I cradle about a dozen or so in the palm of my hand. They're a glistening rainbow of colors, yellow, blue, purple, browns and some reds. I glance up at My Lai and she's pouring us another drink.

"Did you test them," I said.

"No, but I think they're real. Don't you have a test kit?"

"No, but Cathy does. I'll give her a call."

"By the time Cat arrived, we had shredded the box in search of more gems and we'd lined the beauties in thirty-seven rows of ten, a total of three hundred and sixty-seven diamonds. Cat's got her game face on. She disassembles her test kit which consisted of three small test tubes of fluid, a tiny porcelain dish, and an eyedropper. She carefully lays a half-dozen diamonds of various colors in the dish, and using the eyedropper, she retrieves some liquid from one of the test tubes and squirts it on the diamonds. There's an odd smell and some fizzing. She lets it ferment for about twenty seconds then doused the diamonds with another fluid and dried them off with a polish towel that's part of the kit. Reaching inside her jacket pocket, she fondles a jeweler's eye piece and carefully examines each diamond.

"Wow, these three are about a carat and a half, and these four are at least two carats," she claims, as she points at one group, then another.

"Then they're real right?" I asked.

"Ya damn skippy, they're real!"

"Pour Cat a drink!" I shout with joy.

After Cathy takes a good sip of her drink, she starts to jabber, "These have got to be the Thrift Drug Store diamonds, right?"

She looks at us so we return the look and smile like we've just ate someone's pet hamster. "I hope like hell you've got plenty more of these red babies because they're worth a heck of a lot more money."

"What kind of digits are we talking about, Cat?"

"Commercial rates about two to three hundred thou, but try pushing them on a dealer and you'll only get between seventy-five and a hundred thou for the whole shebang. What I wanna know is how did you get 'em and is this all there is?"

Cathy's staring at me and I look at My Lai. My Lai opens a fresh pack of Newports, tapes one out and offers me a cigarette. I wave her off and she lights up.

"While Roxxy was laid up, I was moonlighting. I used my sick leave to skip work and I pulled a couple sleepovers at the Thrift Store."

"Sleepovers?" asked Cat.

"Yeah, I camped out. I went in about a half-hour before closing and I hid in the walk-in cooler between a rack of Budweiser's and some Miller-Lites."

"You're kidding?" I said, but My Lai ignores my comment and taps some cigarette ash into the palm of her right hand, so I find her an ashtray and she continues.

"I do my homework. I always check things out. The manager and his assistant are the last two employees to close the store. There's a security patrol car that checks the perimeter once every hour. The in-house cameras I can bypass, and there are no electronic sensors to worry about unless you're trying to get in through the roof or some other entrance, so I was safe for a least until the next morning."

"What about the diamonds?" asked Cathy. "Where were they and how did you get 'em out?"

"They were exactly where Roxxy and I thought they'd be, the Fabric Shop basement, right next door."

"Okay, so when you got in what did you find?" said Cat with her eyeballs stretched beyond normal.

"I didn't find any canisters or a safe. The gems were locked away in three steel roller cabinets. Each cabinet was about four and a half feet tall and over three feet wide, with six top drawers, two middle drawers and three on the bottom. I picked the locks and 'voila!' Each drawer's felt bedding was covered in stones. It would have taken me a couple days to get an accurate count, but there must have been at least a million stones."

"What! You've got to be kidding!" said Cat.

"The proof is in the pudding, Cat. I could have taken a hundred thousand stones and the owners probably wouldn't have noticed."

"So were the stones mixed or separated?" I ask.

"Yeah, they were separated by color, so what you see here is a little sample of everything."

"When do you plan to go back because when you do, I wanna go with—"

"Hold up a minute!" interrupted Cat. "Me Lie, how in the hell did you get out of there?"

"Easy, same way I came in."

"You stayed in the cooler overnight?"

"Yeah but there's a fan kill switch, so I turned it off right before I went in the storage room and when the store opened I turned it back on. Then I bailed out around nine o'clock this morning."

"Damn, that was risky."

"Not really because I had nothing on me."

"What do you mean you had nothing on you?" I asked.

"I had nothing on me because I planted the diamonds inside the Thrift Store, so when I walked out I was clean."

"Okay, so how'd you get these diamonds out?"

"I walked up to the cashier and paid for them," said My Lai grinning.

"Huh? You're not making any sense!" yelled Cat.

My Lai sucks her teeth, crushes out her cigarette, then twist her mouth from left to right like she's chewing on something nasty. "Look, its real simple. I spent the remainder of the night stashing diamonds in different products and placing them in the rear stack of different shelves. So the proof was in that box of Tampax which I just purchased less than an hour ago."

"You stashed these pretty babies in the store?" I said.

"Yes! That's what I've been saying all along, and there's no need to shout because my hearing is fine."

"You're one crazy bitch," I say to My Lai. "But you're clever like a fox. Cat, let's roll because we need to do some shopping before that Thrift Drug Store closes."

* * *

To hell with stepping out, but being pent up in my apartment for several days, then getting out to shop for diamonds was a hell of a lot more exciting than getting released from county jail.

We entered the Thrift Drug Store at seven-thirty and were out by a quarter to nine, but we were wrong. The closing time was 11:00 p.m. We took all our goods to My Lai's place because we were too excited to drive any further. Besides, I didn't want to take the risk of doing the unravelling at my place because Bones and Wilma were accustomed to stopping by without giving any prior notice. It took two grocery carts to load Cathy's '55' Caddy with everything we had. And it took us three trips from the carport to get everything inside of My Lai's pad. She still didn't have any real furniture so we set all our baggage on the kitchen counter, and our original plan was to use the butcher block table to do our sorting and counting.

Our shopping tag receipt read two hundred and twenty-seven dollars and eighteen cents. My Lai had diamonds stashed in three economy sized boxes of baby pampers, three twenty ounce boxes of Cheerio's and four packs of Scott's dinner napkins. Each package was marked on the bottom with a pink fluorescent pen. We bought a lot of extra stuff that we didn't need just to keep it real and make a late evening shopping spree look like an ordinary routine.

The adrenaline rush of excitement between us was like we'd been electrically shocked. My entire body felt as though it had been doused in some-type-of sexual gel, because my skin felt tingly and prickly all over. We finally decided on borrowing a blanket from the trunk of Cat's Caddy and laid it on the kitchen floor. Then Cat and I tore into the packages with fury until My Lai warned us to be careful and to take our time because she had used a variety of hiding techniques. For example, diamonds were stashed between the layers and folds of the Scott's Napkins, but all we had to do with the Cheerio's is give the box a good shake and almost all the diamonds fell to the bottom of the container. When we were done, there was trash and debris everywhere, and when we completed the count we had a glittering rainbow of fifty-four thousand, nine hundred and sixty-seven diamonds laid out on the butcher block table in several paper plates.

My Lai did the pencil work and Cat worked the calculator.

"Okay, write this down, My Lai," I instructed. "Diamonds, fifty-four thousand total. Sets of three hundred diamonds, dealer's value is seventy-five grand. Cathy, divide three hundred into fifty-four thousand. What did you get?"

"One hundred eighty!" shouted My Lai with lightning speed before Cathy came up with the same figure.

"Cat, multiply that number times seventy-five thousand."

"That equals...you ready for this?"

My Lai and I exchange blank stares. You can hear a pin drop. It's as though we're under water holding our breaths.

"Thirteen Million one hundred thousand dollars!"

I was stunned by what I'd just heard. When I tried to speak I couldn't. All I could do was hiccup. My Lai patted me on the back but the hiccups wouldn't stop until I went over to the sink and gulped down a cup of warm water. By then, My Lai had recalculated Cat's figures, but Cat was a whiz with numbers. Everything was completely accurate.

"So how we doin' the split," inquired Cat, "three, four, or five?"

"Let's keep a four way split for now," I said. "We'll put aside the nine hundred and sixty-seven gems, and that will leave us thirteen thousand five hundred diamonds each. We've got to keep Wilma in the loop, but I'm not sure what to do about Bones just yet."

"But Bones is our most reliable fence," cried Cathy.

"Tru-dat, and he also knows just about every other reliable fence in the Bay Area, maybe the entire West Coast. My Lai, what would you do? Give us some game, girl?"

My Lai doesn't answer me right away. She sucks her teeth and ponders the question for a minute. Then she reaches inside her parka pocket and pulls out her Newports and offers us one. Cat and I both hate menthols but we take one anyway and we all light up and contemplate in smoke.

"We can't trade these rocks for cash. It's too risky and too dangerous. People will talk and word travels fast. We need to do a two-step, or maybe even a three-step," said My Lai.

"Two-step, three-step!" squawked Cat. "What kind of shit is that?"

Cathy didn't get it but I already had a keen idea of what My Lai was saying, "Cat, you know how big business transactions work," I said. "In this case we have to use our imaginations. You know, like Wall Street stuff."

"Oh, you mean like trading stocks for bonds, or commodities for certificates."

"Yeah, sort of like that, but what we have to figure out is this-how, to whom, and what we want to trade for. So ya'll marinate on them thoughts for a minute because I have an idea, but first I need to investigate it. Check-it-out, I'll hold twenty-seven thousand and each of you hold a stash of thirteen thousand five hundred, and we'll split the nine hundred and sixty-seven gems between us. We'll use them for research and we'll meet back here in three or four days. But be careful, because if Bones get wind of what we're doing...well, just remember, Bones ain't always been known to be working with a full deck and if he thinks we're trying to screw him, he's not gonna hesitate to come after us."

"What do you mean," said My Lai, "like shoot first and ask questions later?"

"No. More like, he don't give a fuck. He just shoots ta' kill."

ROXXY

* * *

All of us girls were so hyped, so it was a good thing we lived in different locations. I didn't feel safe with keeping twenty-seven thousand three hundred and twenty-three gem stones inside my penthouse. I stashed twenty-seven thousand of them in a ruined pair of stockings that I found in my glove box. Next, I pulled into a do-it-yourself carwash and gave my Lexus a rinse. Afterwards, I opened the trunk and stuffed my nylons under the matted wheel-well which held my spare tire.

By the time I got back on the road it was 11:00 p.m. and I got a call. Once again it was Ray.

"Hey, pretty nigga. You must have some telepathic skill, cuz I was just thinking about you. What's that music I hear playing?"

"Oh, it's a local Jazz quintet."

"You out clubbin'?"

"No, I'm at Ronnie Lott's sports bar. You in the neighborhood, aren't you?"

"Well, I'm not quite there yet, but I'm fixin' to be. You alone?"

"Of course I'm alone, and I'm so lonely I could cry, cuz I been thinking 'bout my baaay-bay..."

"Quit while you're ahead, Ray, because you're not a contestant for 'The Voice', and I'm not Christina Aguilera."

"Oh, so you're a cold hearted mama-cita, huh? Well, bring your freckled-ass over here to my Bat Cave, woman. Besides, our last episode didn't turn out so swell, and I've got some making up to do."

"Hold that thought, nigga, cuz I'll be there in a blink."

I made a pit stop at Original Joe's, an OG Italian restaurant on the corner of First and San Carlos, just to use the little girls room and freshen up a bit. The hostess didn't mind because I slipped her a tip coming in and another going out. When I arrived at the sports bar, I found Ray's table with no problem, a cozy private booth next to a

80

window in the rear of the place. Ray was casually dressed and his face was flushed from too much booze and sun exposure. He still looked good but I could tell he was high. Before I took a seat across from him, I took a look around.

"What's the matter, Roxxy, you lose something?"

"No, I was just checking."

"Checking?"

"Yeah, checking." The benches were wooden. I finally sat down. "This is a 49er's club, am I right?"

"Last time I checked it was."

"So why are you wearing a Raider's hat?"

Ray reaches up and pulls the silver and black cap from his head, "Damn, Roxxy," he chuckles, "oops, my bad. But hey, ain't nobody care. I got half a dozen different hats I wear from time to time. Besides, I'm a New Orleans Saints fan."

"You're high, Ray. What you been snortin'?"

Ray digs in his leather vest pocket and tosses me a small piece of waxed paper folded up like a kite. "Thanks, but no thanks." I push the bindle away, but then he opens it up and using his fingernail he takes a couple snorts, then closes his eyes, tweaks his nose, and snorts like Miss. Piggy. When he opened his half-moons he's grinning again.

I say, "Good huh?"

"Not bad, pretty mama. You should try some."

"I said, no thanks, remember. But I'll have one of them," I said pointing to his drink.

"Sure you will," he said with a slight slur and feeling all over himself like he was searching for a cigarette. So I offer him one of mine. I even light it for him.

"So, what are we drinkin?"

He raises his glass and examines it like he's not sure what's in it, "Oh, Royal Crown Black."

Bobbie Ray uses his phone to text a bartender named Mario and immediately a short and sultry Portuguese lookin' white girl wearing a man's football jersey with half a dozen gold chains around her throat brings a tray with two glasses, a container of ice, and a quart of booze. Ray hands her a c-note then grabs her by the waist. She kisses his left check, pats him on the neck and smiles. I pretend she's invisible because I'm enjoying my smoke. Then she reaches in her apron pocket, sets an ashtray on the table and leaves.

"By the way, Roxxy, you look marvelous, girl!" shouts Ray.

I instantly knew he was bullshitting me. I'm not the jealous type so I wasn't concerned about the chick. I was wearing a black leather waist coat, a white laced body suit under a pair of denim pants and a pair of jeweled clogs. My hair was up in a nappy Grecian styled bun. I blew a couple smoke rings and looked him in the eye.

"Ray, I got a proposition for you."

"Okay, let's hear it."

"You got any clients that will trade business for ice?"

"Ice?"

"You know, rocks."

"Rocks? You ain't talking to Fred Flintstone, surgah, but what are you trying to say?"

I open my cigarette case and tap out a couple dozen gems onto the serving tray, an assortment of mostly blue diamonds, six reds and a few whites.

"Hmm, looky-here. Now I get it. All that street labeled yak you was using threw me off."

Ray seemed to instantly sober up. I knew he was serious because he stopped smiling.

"How many of these you got for trade, Roxxy?"

"Oh, about twenty million dollars' worth," I say in a whisper, "but I only need about fourteen mil."

"Fourteen mil for twenty mil in ice? Hmm, that's pretty generous. So my take would be six?"

"You can get whatever if you know how to flip it."

"I got mucho connects, Roxxy, but what are you bartering for, hop, cola—"

"Hemp."

"Mary Jane?"

"Yeah, her."

Bobbie Ray nods his head up and down several times. He's contemplating and he reminds me of a bobble head doll. I can't help but giggle.

"Who else besides you is in on it?"

"It's cool Ray. Me and my crew are tight."

"How many?"

"There's three of us."

"Well, I hope ya'll like to fly."

"Fly?"

"Yeah, like Cayman Islands, maybe."

"Why there?"

"Because, you'll need to open up a few off-shore accounts."

"Can't we do that on the internet?"

"I wouldn't advise it."

"How long is all this gonna take?"

"From start to finish, about two to three months. We'll have to do it in installments."

"Okay, I can live with that." I reach inside my blouse and remove a wad of plastic from under my bra and hand it to Ray, "Here's your starter kit."

"How many is in here."

"A little over three hundred."

"What's the rate?"

"The low is a hundred thou and the high is two-hundred and fifty thou."

"What's the carat average?"

"It varies between one to two and a half."

"They been tested?"

"Of course, but I'm sure your people will want to do their own test, so do whatever you gotta do."

"Okay, I'll get back to you within a week. Tell your crew to be ready and pack a bag."

* * *

All that shop talk excited me but exhausted me as well. Ray and I made earth-shaking love, and by 1:00 a.m. I was pulling up at my penthouse. Twenty minutes later, it was lights out and my hutch was closed.

CHAPTER SEVEN

Elmo

MY MOMMA ONCE told me to never count my chickens before they've hatched and I tried doing that for most of my life but for some reason I woke up the next morning with that same queasy feeling I've felt from the start of this caper.

After a five-minute stretch, a quick shower, toast and a latte, me and Mugsy took our usual morning run. The almost summer like air was a little damp. The sky was a mix of faded magenta and blue. I felt it was going to be another warm day. On my return trip home I stopped by my favorite magazine and cigar store and picked up a Cosmopolitan, an Ebony, and a USA Today. Then I dropped Mugsy off at a doggie care center where he'd get Ritz Carlton doggie treatment, bath, grooming, and kick it with a few other mutts for the entire day.

Home at last, I took another shower and fixed myself a skillet of fried rice with eggs, cheese grits, a fried green tomato, and a fat dill pickle. After eating all of that, I still wasn't quite full. I cleaned up the kitchen and had myself a kronut and a glass of milk as I read the papers and relaxed in my Lazyboy chair. When my phone chimed, instantly I knew it was Cat.

"Hey Roxanne, how you doin ?"

"I'm doin'. Hey, you got any 'Butt-naked's?"

"Butt-naked's?"

"Yeah, 'Butt-naked's."

"Nah, but I guess I could get some from Tommy Boy if you're serious."

"I'm just clowning, girl. You Know I don't mess with crack. So, what-up? Why are you calling me so early?"

"Early? "

"Yeah, early, and do you have to always repeat a question with the same question, like you old or somethin'?"

"Look who's talkin'. You do it all the time and I never complain."

"Tru-dat, so why aren't you out running the streets yet?"

"Because, I've been listening to the a.m. Newscast. Turn on your T.V. Change it to channel seventy-seven and check out the ticker at the bottom of the screen."

I grab my remote and power up, "Okay, it's on. What am I looking for?"

"It's on sports right now...shit!, now they done went to a commercial."

"Well-hell, just tell me what I'm supposed to be watching."

"The Thrift Drug Shopping Center has been burglarized."

"Burglarized?"

"See, there you go, repeating what I just said. Yeah, the newscaster said someone got into their safe and stole some undisclosed amounts of money and jewels."

"Come-on, Cat. Are you serious or just trying to fuck with my emotional mojo?"

"Look the news is back on, check for yourself."

I didn't want to believe what I was reading from the ticker, then hearing it repeated by the newscaster. I was in shock and my eyeballs wouldn't move.

"Cat, are you still there?"

"Yeah, you can hear me can't you?"

"Of course, but are you thinking like I'm thinking?"

"What do you mean, that maybe we've been played?"

"I'm not sure, but we haven't got enough info to make that call, but hold on a minute."

I called My Lai but I got her voice mail.

"Cat! "

"What?"

"My Lai's not answering her phone."

"So."

"So, I'm calling her place of work."

"Okay, go head but click me in"

"Brinks Incorporate, how may I help you?"

"Yes, can I leave a message for one of your employees?"

"Sure. What's the name?"

"My Lai Smith, she's a guard."

Seconds later, "Maim, there's no one who works here by that name."

"Ahh, I'm not sure of the last name. How about just, My Lai." I had to spell it for her but it still didn't help.

"Roxanne!"

"Yeah."

"Maybe you should have asked for Lucy Lui."

"Fuck you, Cat. Don't play with me because I'm pissed right now!"

"Aw, Roxanne, we still go a good chunk of ice. If she burnt us for the rest, why fret, cuz it ain't nothin' but a shrimp thing."

"A shrimp thing! Hell-no, Cat! If she took it all then that's a double cross! We crossed Bones and now she's crossing us. Besides, we don't even know for certain if the diamonds are the real deal."

"Have you forgotten that I tested them?"

"No, you tested some, not all. Think about it. My Lai didn't go shopping with us last night. She told us what items were marked and where to look while she watched us, probably with binoculars, from her front room window."

"Damn, Roxanne, you may be right, cuz we were so anxious to get in and get out that we didn't take time to disguise ourselves—"

"So we're on film and she's not."

"Motha' fuck!"

"And that bullshit story she told me about Bones and her dad serving time together—"

"She did? You didn't tell me about that."

"It don't matter. The fact remains that after we split up last night she went back in some other way and got everything she left behind, probably close to a million diamonds if that part is true. And once she got ghost, she didn't give a shit about tripping an alarm."

"But check-it-out, we still might be in the clear, because to some private dick on the outside looking in, we're just shoppers. So we know all the pieces to the puzzle and so does My Lai. Even if she skyed on us, we just gotta chill and play dumb, whether its Bones doing the asking or anyone else."

"That sneaky hefa', I'm a choke that bitch mentally. She thinks she's nickel-slick. She betta' be talking to a priest and saying her last prayers, cuz if half the diamonds we got aren't real, then I'mma help Bones hunt her sleazy ass down."

"Chill-out, Roxanne, we ain't loss nothing but a little less cheddar."

"Why do you keep saying that?"

"Imitation rocks are expensive to make and we got forty thousand five hundred of 'em. So we can sell them out of state with no questions asked."

Listening to what Cat had to say made me feel a little better but there were still a lot of unanswered questions, like if we were being screwed, then who was actually doing the screwing, Bones or My Lai. Or maybe, they were on the same team and working me and Cat like a rib sandwich.

* * *

I could never have been a dope fiend because I hate the waiting game. If I got money and the shit ain't ready, then I'm kicking somebody's door down just to find out what the hell's taking so long. Wow, 'the committee' is throwing a party inside my head. These thoughts I'm having must belong to somebody else because they surely aren't mine. For the past four days, me and Cathy ain't heard a peep out of nobody. No calls from Bag of Bones-Bones, Wilma nor Sara Lee, ole' shady-ass bitch. Ooou, how I hate being played!

I tried to keep my mind off of shit that I have no power over. In this instance, all I can do is keep busy and wait. In the meantime, I booked a dozen dates with the usual clientele. I even picked up a couple decent new referrals. On the fifth day, after all the rumbles in the hotel-bedroom-jungles ceased, I gave Miss. Kenny a call.

"Hello, Kenny Jackson?"

"Yee-ah."

"This is Roxanne, surgah'."

Kenny's voice didn't have that natural cheerful ring I had become accustomed to. Right away I knew something wasn't right.

"Ooou Roxanne, I'm glad you called. Bobbie Ray gave me a number that you can reach him at but I'm too weak right now to look for it."

"Weak? What's the matter, Kenny, have you come down with somethin'?"

"Nooo."

"Well, I want to come and see you and spend some time with you. Besides, maybe I can help you find that number. Is that okay?"

"I guess so...yeah, come over."

"Okay, so give me your address. Are you still living in Berkeley?"

"Yee-ah, but right now I'm staying in an apartment in Santa Cruz."

"Okay-good, that's even closer. I'll be there within the hour."

Kenny's apartment complex was three blocks from the University of Santa Cruz. After speaking to him through a squawk-box, a flick of his security buzzer allowed me to come in. His apartment was on the second floor. The door was opened so I walked right in.

"Kenny, I'm here. It's me, Roxanne," I said in a sing-song voice. I entered the tiny room with caution. There was a stale musty odor so as soon as I closed the door, I cranked open a window and let in some sunlight and fresh air. Kenny never moved. All I could see was the top of his scalp, and his little forehead was peppered with beads of sweat. He was buried in five blankets. Again, I called out to him. This time he stirred with a slight moan, then turned his back to me. So immediately I knew what to do.

The room resembled a college dorm. Not a place you'd expect a rich kid to be living in, although the studio was very neat and clean. It had a tiny private bathroom area with a kitchenette that was shared with a next door neighbor. I turned the heater off. It was ten o'clock in the morning and already seventy degrees outside. Then I boiled a kettle of water and made lemon tea and found a canister of pop-open dinner rolls in the fridge. I hoped they were his because it took less than five minutes to cook them in a microwave. In the meantime, I filled his sink with cool water, took the pile of blankets off him and got him to sit up. His body temperature was warm but he didn't have a fever. The little man was just depressed. A woman's caring touch was the only remedy I had. I hoped it would work on him. I bathed his chest but he wouldn't let me touch anything below. I watched him sip his tea as the redness in his beautiful brown fawn eyes began to clear. I went through his dresser drawer and gave him fresh clothing and as soon as I turned my head, he made a dash for the shower. I didn't look and didn't talk.

Once he toweled himself dry and changed clothes, he looked and smelled a lot better. I had him sit on a stool and he ate jelly buttered rolls while I untangled his naps and braided his hair. Kenny had gnarly rope-like Indian hair. I twisted four fat braids which almost touched his shoulders then he finally spoke.

"Oh, Roxanne, thank you for coming to see about me. I feel much better now."

His mouth was stuffed with dough and with his Elmo voice it made him sound extra funny.

"What's wrong Kenny, why are you living alone like this? It's not your style, honey. Tell me what's ailing you."

"I've fallen in love with a straight man, Roxanne."

"Houston?"

"Yeah, an that was a big mistake, cuz now I'm gone off him-"

"And he's not feeling the same way about you?"

"Noooo..." Kenny begins to cry real big crocodile tears.

"Oh, Kenny, you should know better. When it comes to straight men, honey, they're just in it for the sex. They'll flip on you without a moment's notice."

"Ooooh, but I never knew being in love with someone could hurt so bad."

"So what happened, honey?" Kenny's nose is running. I help him dry his cheeks as he looks up at me. He still reminds me of Elmo, but he's hurting so no time for jokes. I dare not laugh.

Kenny continues, "I let him have my booty."

"Oh..." was all I could think to say.

"Yeah, I've never done that for any man, gay or straight. So I got sprug and I think he liked it too. We were doing it every day and everywhere for a while. He told me I was the best he ever had and he was thinking about me all the time."

"And you interpreted that as being in love with you, right?"

"Yes, because it had to be real. I could feel it in my fingers, toes, and every part of my little body. His love just took over me. I wanted him so, and I felt proud to have him as my man and I wanted the whole world to know it."

"So, if everything was going so well, what changed it?"

"Ronnie told me he saw Houston coming out the back of his van with someone else."

"Who?"

"With Fancy. Fancy is real cute and he's built like a natural woman. He can get any straight man he wants because he has been taking estrogen tablets and hormone shots since he was a teenager."

"Oh, so you know him?"

"Yes-I-do!"

"Well, have you confronted him about it?"

"No, I asked Houston but he told me it wasn't true. But Ronnie and I have been friends for eons. The only reason he told me is because he doesn't want to see me get hurt, but I'm hurt anyway."

Kenny began to tremble then he shut his eyes tight then opened them again. I didn't know whether to believe him or not. I'm sure he had practice at pretending to be the victim. It was easy for him to lie. It wasn't like I could check his hymen to see if his virginity was intact. "Kenny, listen to me," I grabbed him by his shoulders and looked him in the eyes, "You've got to let this relationship with Houston go before it causes you any more pain. Look, you made a mistake. You fell in love with the wrong guy. No man like that is worth making you feel miserable."

"Roxanne, you don't understand. I'm not gonna let that Jezebel take Houston from me, because Fancy is only gonna hurt him just so she can brag about stealing a straight guy from me."

"But if you know that then you must not bite into Fancy's shenanigans. You've got to play it cool, Kenny, and at least pretend for now that it doesn't have any effect on you. Sooner or later Houston will figure Fancy out and come to his senses. He'll come back to you if he really cares about you."

"You really think so, Roxanne?"

"Surga', trust me, he'll be back beggin'. Just give the situation a little more time, and in the meantime, you got plenty of men that want to be with you. Snag one of them and let Houston see the two of you hanging out and having a good time.

"Thanks, Roxanne. I like that plan, because I believe it will work."

"Good, so let's find what I came here for."

"Oh, I plumb forgot. Bobbie Ray's number."

* * *

I liked Miss. Kenny, but now I'm really worried about him. Catching a straight man is a huge status symbol for gays of Kenny's caliber. I hope Houston is being for real about his feelings toward Lil' Kenny and not just being some sexaholic who's woken up from being momentarily sprung.

I was never able to reach Ray even with the new number but by the weeks end Karrene called and told me that since I was doin so well with my probation, the courts agreed to give me an early discharge. Now that was worth a celebration. So by the time Friday arrived I had conjured up some party plans, when suddenly Cathy came barging in that late afternoon. She had a wide-eyed wild look and she was definitely in a huff.

"Sit down and relax yourself, Cat, before you pass out."

I mixed her a drink.

"What did you do, run all the way down here from your apartment?"

She used her finger to stir the ice in her rum and coke and took a sip, "No, but I rushed over as fast as I could."

I made a funny face, "Why?"

"Well, I made a pit stop over at Bag of Bones pool hall. You know we haven't heard from him or Wilma in a while."

"Okay...so what about it?"

"Well, when I got there the place was on lock-down. It had one of those signs plastered on the door talking about seizure of liquor license and forbidden sale to minor...yahda, yahda, yahda. So I peeked through the glass and saw chairs piled atop of pool tables and a few overhead lamps were left on. You know Bones would never leave his place in disarray like that."

"Okay, so the place looked deserted."

"Yeah, so I dashed over to the corner of Fourth and Saint James and ran into Tommy Boy. You know that's his spot where he handles his business."

"Yeah, I know. He sells pills, meth, crack, and just about everything else."

"Right."

"So what did you find out?"

"Tommy Boy says that Wilma and Bones got sloppy drunk one night and the next morning ran off to Vegas to get married."

"Married?"

"Don't ask me. I'm just telling you what the man said."

"Humph, that's odd."

"Yeah, I agree but check this out."

Cat hands me her cell.

"Go to Yahoo and click on Gazette. It's a Las Vegas newspaper blog."

I follow Cat's instructions and the first thing I see glaring back at me is bold black block letters..."NEWLYWEDS CREATE SUICIDE PACT". I scroll down and a picture of a female in a wedding dress is standing next to some guy in a tuxedo. I click the cell's zoom button twice, then three more times and damn near drop the phone when I realize what I'm looking at is a picture of Wilma Sarpy and Bag of Bones-Bones.

"Cat, are you sure this isn't a hoax?" I say as I speed read the article. "This has got to be a joke," I babble.

Cat's got that Oprah Winfrey without make-up look on her face.

"You're scaring me, Cat, speak up!"

"Hell, I don't know Roxanne. Tommy Boy said he thinks it's a hit made to look like suicide."

"A HIT!"

"Yeah, apparently Bones was in some serious debt with a couple bookies out of Vegas. Tommy Boy says he overheard a conversation while Bones had him monitoring the door during a backroom meeting. Bones was planning a big heist to cover the debt but it didn't happen due to some bogus information. The deal fell through and Bones' time limit for payment had run out. I think he was forced to return to Vegas to try and re-negotiate the debt. So as you just read, they found them in the front seat fully dressed with a hose attached to the tail-pipe that was snaked through a backseat passenger's side window."

Now I could see why Cathy was looking like she was about to cry as this creepy prickly feeling ran through my tall-ass body. The room began to spin so I had to sit down.

"Cat."

"What?"

"We're in a heap of shit honey," I say, as Cathy walks over to my bar and pours us a straight shot of Jack Daniels whiskey. I take a gulp. My eyes are already blurry so it doesn't help.

"We gotta find that winch, My Lai," said Cat, "before them Las Vegas hoodlums do."

"I know-I know, because if they get her to talk, then they'll be coming after us. Besides, we don't know what kind of deal Bones contracted with them," I said.

"You're right, and the main question is, before they died were they forced to give up some names."

"Maybe, but how in the hell are we supposed to locate My Lai when she done vanished like Casper the Ghost?"

"I don't have an answer for that," said Cat.

"Well, I do. Let's take Bobbie Ray's advice and pack a bag."

"Pack a bag?"

"Yeah, cuz it's a good time to travel and see the sights."

* * *

As luck would have it, I tried that unlucky number and touchdown! It was Ray who answered the phone.

"It's about time you got back at me, Roxxy. Why are you so hard to keep track of?"

"Meeee?"

"You're crazy, woman. I'mma make this short 'cause I don't like discussing business over the phone, so listen up. Everything is legit and ready to roll. You ready to travel?"

"It's your call, Ray, but I'm short."

"By how much?"

"By a fourth."

"Well, I can still get you fifteen if you and your crew can accept nine."

With time being an issue I wasn't in a position to haggle. It was a win-win situation. But I wasn't sure if the money was important enough to risk me and Cathy Wilson's life.

* * *

CHAPTER EIGHT

Barracuda

ON SATURDAY, CATHY Wilson and I took a Boeing 777 out of San Francisco International at 11:00 a.m. and landed on a Miami air strip two hours passed noon. From there, we took a shuttle over these bridges that seemed to be headed for the edge of the earth until we reached the island of Key West, where the huge orange sun seemed to melt into the sea. A twin engine Cessna took us to the Bahamas. We touched down in Nassau around 9:00 p.m. Eastern Standard time. We had our choice of plush hotels, Hyatt, Hilton, you name it, the American influence and tourists were everywhere. We settled on the Paradise Hotel. It came highly recommended and it was owned by a Brit. After unpacking we were too tired to do anything but sleep.

We spent our last week in the South Bay placing stuff in storage and leaving messages with only a few friends and telling them we'd be out of town for at least a month. Cat had to leave her Caddy in her mechanic's San Mateo storage. I hated leaving Mugsy but I had a neighbor who was happy to keep him until my return. Of course, Mugsy knew something was up. He latched on to my calf and wouldn't let go. I guess he figured if he held onto my leg long enough he wouldn't get left behind.

Our first morning in Nassau began a lot earlier than we expected. Room service arrived at 6:00 a.m. We had breakfast and we hit the pavement somewhere between 7:00 and 8:00 a.m. People of color were everywhere. They waited on us like we were American diplomats or long lost relatives from the Ivory Coast. Them ninjas were serious about hustling a monk, but it was okay. We didn't mind being spoiled with attention. They did a lot of smiling and carrying on. They convinced us we needed a guide. Their accents were rich and thick, a mix of African, British, and French. It didn't take long before me and Cat was mimicking them.

Ray arrived on a noon flight. He had already called and checked in with us twice. By mid-afternoon he had three million dollars wired to two different banks under two new aliases with credentials. Ray instructed us that it was important we memorize our new bank account numbers rather than write them down. Lucky for us, Cat and I had a knack for keeping numbers in our head. Then he opened up a black canvas gym bag that he was carrying and dumped twenty-five bundles of cash onto our couch.

"You're looking at about two hundred and fifty grand of mostly large bills," said Ray grinning. "Divide it up cuz it should be enough to get you by for a couple weeks and maybe a month since there's only two of you. What happened to the third leg?"

Cathy and I looked at each other and just shrugged our shoulders and Ray got the hint. He frowned but continued, "Well, don't spend it all in one place. Besides, you'll need to hire a private boat captain so you can island hop."

"Island hop!" I protested. "Come-on, Ray, what's the hold up, honey? How long is it gonna take before all of our money gets here?"

Ray shrugged his broad shoulders then threw his palms up like he thought I might try to box with him, "Ease up Roxxy! I'm not Warren Buffet and these transactions may take a couple of weeks to complete. In the meantime, you and Cathy need to make yourselves comfortable and act like tourist."

"You mean kick back and take in the sights?" added Cat.

"Exactly, learn your way around, and once all your money is in place, then you can decide what your next move should be."

"I don't know, Ray, cuz I'm not use to being around all this water."

"Ha! Me neither," agrees Cathy. "I'm anxious to get back to the States cuz I can't swim."

"What are you worried about?" counters Ray. "This ain't even hurricane season."

"Sheee-it, that may be true but what if one of them big-ass tsunamis shows up?"

Bobbie Ray, can't hold back a grin that turns into a chuckle, "Well, maybe it's a good time for the two of you to start taking swimming lessons."

"In these waters? No-way!" snaps Cat.

"Okay-then, my bad, but when you meet Jimmy, he'll help you overcome all your phobias, crazy-ass woman."

"Who's Jimmy?" I ask.

"Jimmy is the bartender over at the Paradise Hotel. He knows everything there is to know about the islands in the Caribbean. He's gonna be looking out for you while I'm gone for the next couple weeks."

"What's he charging?"

"I don't know his rates, Cathy, but rest assured, he's not gonna fleece you."

* * *

Jimmy's homeland was the island of Saint Croix, around forty miles southeast of Barbados and two hundred and fifty miles north of South America's Venezuela. Nassau being the capitol of the Bahamas was situated on the Island of Andros. Andros was not only a haven for tourist but, businessmen and women throughout the world. It was in Nassau that islanders like Jimmy could find work or perhaps launch a career. Jimmy came from a typical island family who were either fisherman, boat builders, or farmers. It was a common thread of their culture which over time had become influenced by the drug trade, gun running, and many other illicit schemes that seemed to nourish in some parts of the

Caribbean. Jimmy was skilled and experienced at almost every facet of the game and was one of Bobbie Ray's most trusted cohorts, and because of that he was able to make a ton of money for himself.

Cat and I first laid eyes on Jimmy at a big food vendor's market, a popular tourist spot on the islands north shore which was situated in bungalows along a sandy white beach. Jimmy had an athletic build, shoulder length dreads, and rough skin blackened by the sun. He had a comely and persistent smile, narrow brown friendly eyes, and a resonating husky voice. He told everyone we met that we were his American sisters. We stuck to him like glue. Jimmy knew everything there was to know about boats, yachts, and cat rams. He also advised us on the areas daily ritual and little history of the island folks.

"I've known Bobbie for a good bit," said Jimmy with a British accent, "A Jonnah, he's not', so you're lucky to have the clink for a mate'. Trust me when I say, I've never known him to be a silly arse' nor a swizz' or a wag."

I tug at Cathy's sleeve, "What did he just say Cat?"

"He said, Bobbie Ray is trustworthy and outstanding and he's not the foolish type."

"Oh."

"I hope you bints—"

Cat and I both frown.

"I mean, ladies are not weeds--"

"Weeds? What's a weed?" I ask.

Jimmy clears his throat, "A weak person, a weakling."

"Oh, you mean easy," I say.

"Yeah, kind of like that but I hope not, because if you are, you might get dickie- bowed by the sharks in these waters."

"Sharks!" cried Cat.

"No, not the fishy kind, Ms. Cathy, I'm talking about the two-legged kind. They smell money like its blood. So the two of you need not to go flashin' your wears too brightly in the hotels and casinos. For you may get shanghai'ed and sold to the biggest baller. An' if you're unable to amply supply your kidnapper's lust, they'll not hesitate to chop you into chum and use you for bait."

Jimmy's straight talk made us feel a little more leery of the unfamiliar yet exotic surroundings, "Since you're our escort then we shouldn't have anything to worry about, right Cat?" I nudge her with my elbow.

"Yeah, we grown-ass women in case you didn't notice," says Cat thrusting out her chest and posing like Wonder Woman with hands on both hips. She's staring back at Jimmy like he's got rocks in his mouth. I don't think she likes him. Jimmy gives her the shine and keeps talking.

"You'll spend four to seven days at each island then move on. Tomorrow you'll leave Nassau and sail for Abaco, and from there Eliuthera, and if necessary, the Great Inagua Island."

"How much do you expect to get paid for being our escort?" I asked.

"I'm your cabbie for now, but my cousin owns the vessel that will take you where you need to go. He'll want a twenty-five hundred dollar retainer and he charges three hundred per day. He will give you quarters and assign you a cabin girl and a cook. On Abaco as well as the other islands, you will have a bungalow overlooking you own private beach. The rent is three thousand a week, but a few days stay will ensure you a negotiable rate."

Jimmy, the court jester, was me and Cathy's dinner date at the Paradise Hotel. The food was fabulous but we ate too much. Tomorrow we'd have a long day ahead of us, so we bypassed the night club circuit. About an hour after unwinding and finally getting to bed, I still couldn't sleep. My stomach was feeling queasy again. So I drank a warm glass of milk and took a quick cool shower. This time I washed my hair and the remedy worked. I went back to bed and drifted into one dream and then another...The stream of dreams was pleasant at first, but they eventually turned ugly and woke me up. An hour later, I drifted into sleep for the second time...

I don't know where the morbid thoughts came from. I know it was overpowering and it wouldn't go away. If I had not seen the skull and cross-bone label on the bottle, perhaps the thoughts wouldn't have entered my mind. My mom killed herself with arsenic. I barely remember because I was only eight, but I recall her sprinkling a little spoon of white powder over almost every meal she ate, right before saying grace... The bottle I was looking at was small. The poison was green, translucent, and thick. It was an ant syrup of some kind, "I HAD NO DOUBTS I WOULD NOT FAIL THIS TIME", a voice inside me said. Camouflaging the hideous smell was a problem. I decide on mixing it in a malted shake to help wash it down.

The concoction became an inferno inside my stomach and I had an eruption of the worst kind. The pain was excruciating. Once the regurgitation began I couldn't stop.

I threw up again and again.

I was vomiting particles of my intestinal lining when suddenly some snake like creature burst through my navel, oozed and slithered over my naked breast and was headed for my face.

I couldn't breathe!

I was in a catatonic state.

The thing from my belly had no eyes and it was trying to smother me.

I no longer could see it but I knew it was there.

I struggled to escape.

I banged my head and woke up...

I yanked away the bed sheets that were covering my face. I took a deep breath and tossed them under the bed.

* * *

I turned on the bedside lamp and lit a cigarette. Shadows from the whirl of the overhead fan gave the room a sinister feel. I felt defenseless and weak. I was alone and my thoughts went to Ray. There was a chance his flight could have been delayed, so I gave him a call.

"What up," he answered.

"It's me, Ray!"

"Roxxy?"

"Yeah, nigga. Are you in the air yet?"

"No, we had a flight delay. It should be cleared up by—"

"I need you, Ray."

"What--"

"I need you here, right now!"

That's one thing I liked about Bobbie Ray. He knew when not to ask a woman a lot of questions. He was knocking on my door an hour before the sun came up. I'd taken another shower and put on a fresh negligee and some perfume. One of my neighbors, an early riser, was playing Caribbean calypso music. The lyrics came streaming through my window as soon as I answered the door...

[Music] Tell me you love me boy...

The lustful way you use to say, you love me more day by day...

Tell me you love me boy...

The way you use to talk to me, when our love was new.

It's a long-long time, since you've held me in your arr-arms..

Oooo-oou the words you say every day, sweet-sweet thing-ings...

Ray brought a bottle of champagne. I watched him pop the cork and pour us each a glass. We sipped and stared at one another, and it was as if we were seeing each other for the first time. Then my neighbor's stereo played another song. This one was a sultry tune, "I Wish You Belong to me" I didn't recognize the singer's voice.

[Music) Here we are meeting again...

Sipping champagne just like friends...

I can see the sparkle in your eyes...

But everyone knows, I'm not your guy...

Wish that you could be—long—to me--—ee.

As we listened, Ray led me to a rattan couch and had me sit down. Then he kneeled before me and gently spread my legs and poured champagne on my thighs. Looking down at him, all I could see in the dimly lit room was his shiny face and moist curly locks of hair. He removed his leather jacket and unbuttoned his shirt. I reached down and ran my fingers through his hairy chest. Ray kissed my fingers, slid his palms under my buttocks, and before I could catch my breath his hot mouth was pressed against my pussy. Teasing my labials with his nose and tongue, he moistened me until he found my clit. Then he taunted it with his tongue by gently rubbing underneath then sucking it again...I released a low moan as he repeated the process, rubbing, squeezing and nibbling again and again...

Once my shivering began, it wasn't but a moment before I erupted. I creamed in lathers. Ray looked so sweet with beads of perspiration cascading down his forehead and dripping off his nose. I clamped my thighs around his shoulders and he lapped me like a newborn getting his momma's milk.

Men love being in control and I wasn't accustomed to being taken, but I wasn't faking. My orgasms were real. It didn't matter if Ray loved me or not. I knew I could never take his wifey's place, his number one. I just wanted him to care about me and fuck me good.

* * *

PART II

CHAPTER NINE

Agent Orange

IN THE SOUTHBAY, My Lai's (me-lie's) Thrifty Drug heist was an on-going investigation, not only by the cops, but by an insurance company as well. Etna Insurance.

Etna Insurance Company hired Sunset Investigations as an outside source. I didn't find this out until much later and I also didn't know that the owner of Sunset Investigations was Bobbie Ray's kid brother-Rob Cash and his girlfriend Ashley Jensen.

* * *

"Hey Kitten, we better get going, cuz you're gonna make us late!"

"Kitten? Oh, so now I'm your 'kitten' since you want me to hurry up?"

"It's only a term of endearment, Ashley. No need to go into commando mode on me."

I'm not, Robbie, but I'm just sayin', you use to call me 'pumpkin' and on occasion 'babe', so I've gone from being a vegetable to an infant and now I'm suppose to be a kitty cat!"

"Whoa-whoa, stop. Hey, I apologize." Rob takes a deep sigh and turns around to look at Ashley. "My bad, Ashley. Just know that I'm proud to have you as my woman, and I'm glad that you watch my back because you've proven yourself to be a top notch P.I. It's because of you and our teamwork that the county gave our agency the Top Investigators Award."

"I know, Robbie, and we deserved it, cuz we never give up on a case.

"That's true, now if we don't get going we're gonna be late. So let's roll, Kitten."

"Robbie, you're despicable!" said Ashley with a snicker.

They arrived at the Thrifty Drug Shopping Center parking lot in Rob's Subaru Tribeca. It's been two months since the diamond heist. The Patel Family's loss was estimated around 50 million dollars. At least that's what the gem stones had been insured for. It was Etna Insurance who hired Rob and Ashley to assist with the investigation because their own agents had already run out of leads. Etna's chief investigator, Anthony Moore, a short and gabby wise-ass, who always had to have the last word, turned a lot of heads because he looked like a famous comedian.

After Rob and Ashley parked, Agent Moore spotted the pair of P.I.'s as he paced back and forth on the sidewalk that fronted the mall. Without haste, he ran over and greeted them.

"You ready to put in some work?"

"You bet Mr. Moore."

"Slow down, Robbie," replied Ashley, "not without having me some coffee."

"No problem," snapped the agent, "I'm one step ahead of ya. I've got the coffee brewing as we speak. But just a reminder, my associates call me Shawty."

"Okay, Mr. Shawty," countered Rob, "but has anybody ever told you that you look like a famous comedian?"

Agent Moore cringes, "Fuck-no, Cash! An' don't ever compare me to that idiot again! You understand what I'm sayin', son?"

"Eh, my mistake," said Rob trying his best not to laugh because Agent Moore was looking back at him with a goofy scowl.

The threesome entered the Thrift Drug Store's front entrance doorway. It was Friday, around ten in the morning, and the sky was pale blue. Outside, the temperature reached a mild sixty-five. The store was already bustling with customer's shopping as the agents made a bee-line for the cooler of beverages, and Agent Moore, using his own keys, unlocked the storage that led them down a stairway and through a short tunnel. Unlocking another door, they reached the room that once held the multi-million dollar stones.

"Okay gang, welcome to our 'chat room'. Everything you need is set up right here at your fingertips, forty-eight inch touch screen, computerized monitor loaded with a history of employee files and surveillance footage. Ashley, there's your coffee and vending machines filled with sandwiches and refreshments, free of charge, complements of the Patel's. Oh, and I almost forgot," said the little man before heading for the exit, "here's your personal set of storage room keys and my cell number in case you need something. The place is all yours."

"Where are you going?" huffs Ashley.

"Who me?" said the agent with a look of amusement as he points an index finger at himself. "I got a lead I need to follow up on, but don't worry I won't be far. I'll check back with you later."

Agent Moore glanced at his wrist watch he wore facing palm-up and said, "See ya!"

"Ha-ha!" laughs Rob. "It looks like Agent Shortdog is leaving us with all the work, Kitten."

"Humph, he's a real Waldo, Robbie, but we gotta be careful what we say around him, cuz he's kinda like our supervisor and we don't want him getting us fired. Besides, with all this film footage, we're bound to find some good clues as to who might have pulled this robbery.

"Hey, that's my girl and I'm with you on that note," replied Rob as he begins rolling up his shirt sleeves.

* * *

Agent Moore, Etna Insurance's chief investigator, had been working in the field for more than sixteen years. He was a shrewd investigator but he also had a reputation for roughing up clients and violating their constitutional rights. He did whatever it took to close a case. Driving his black XJ8 Jaguar, he zipped out of the parking lot and took the 280 Freeway towards downtown San Jose. He found a vacant metered parking slot at Twenty-Eleven South 2nd Street. Then he took a slow walk over to a hooker who was leaning against the doorway of an old three story hotel.

"Hello there! You working today?"

"You see me standin' here don't you, so what do it look like?"

Agent Moore ignores the hooker's snide comment, "Look, I got a C-note for you if you'll have breakfast with me and answer a few questions."

"I'm not hungry!" blurts the hooker.

"Okay, how about if I throw in another twenty?"

The hooker hikes up her already short skirt and sneaks a peak over the agent's shoulder, "Throw in a couple more of them twenties and you got yourself a date but only for a half an hour."

"Alright, but let's get moving cause we're wasting valuable time."

They walk for half a block and step into Pepe's, a tiny Mexican mom and pop restaurant. Agent Moore eats there on occasions. He's a valued repeat customer, so the waitress serves the couple with the VIP treatment. Agent Moore orders Juevos Rancheros, steak and eggs, but first comes the nacho chips, a bowl of salsa, and two bottles of Dos Equis, a dark Mexican beer.

The hooker makes herself comfortable in the mini-booth's seat. She's sitting directly across from Agent Moore. The restuarant's grill orders makes the room a little warm so the hooker unbuttons her sweater to reveal a pink ruffled blouse and the deep cleavage of her forty plus bosom. Agent Moore tries to avoid staring at her tits but she catches his feeble attempt at sneaking a peak.

"You see something you like?" said the hooker releasing a coy smile. "I know your not a cop so what are you...a lawyer, a banker--"

"I'm a life insurance salesman, if you must know, Miss.--"

"Crystal...you can call me, Crystal."

"Okay, Crystal. You know a street walker that goes by the name 'Candy Cane ?

"I might. What about her?"

"Well, I know for a fact that this area use to be her 'stroll'...you know what I mean?"

Crystal gave Agent Moore a blank stare and said nothing.

"Do you have any idea where I might find her at this time of day?"

"Nope...Candy and me ain't in the same league, so we ain't got no reason to hang out."

"Oh, why's that?"

"Cuz she don't need to walk the streets anymore. She's got her own private clientele, so she ain't gotta deal with tricks like you."

"I'm not a 'trick', Miss. Crystal."

"Oh, is that so. Humph, well I seen the way you was looking down my cleavage and I ain't charging you for that, but if you let me show you my Pricilla, you gon' definitely want some of that."

Crystal gives Agent Moore a smeared lipstick commercial smile. Her dimpled cheeks are an oily cocoa brown and she's wearing a strawberry blond wig, so she looks kinda cute, or at least she thinks she does.

"Pricilla? Hmm..." is all that the agent can say. He's obviously amused. "I might take you up on that if you help me find where Miss. Candy's flat is located."

Crystal reaches under the table and grabs Agent Moore by the crotch of his trousers. His eyes bulge and with a knee jerk reaction he bangs the table. Then his head swivels as he takes a quick look around the room to see if anyone's watching.

Crystal giggles softly to herself. She's a keen observer of human nature, so she doesn't let go. She rubs his dick as it snakes through his pants. Now she knows the type of car the insurance salesman drives and the Felmar, Ulysse Nardin watch he's wearing speaks money. Those two items are worth about a hundred and fifty grand alone. But Crystal is on the clock and doesn't want her pimp to lose patience with her, so she bounces out of the restaurant while Agent Moore takes a restroom break. Before leaving, she jots down her private cell phone number on a napkin and slides it under the breakfast plate.

Moments later, with a toothpick resting in the corner of his mouth, Agent Moore takes another slow walk to where his Jaguar is parked. He notices an unsavory looking guy watching him from across the crowded streets. When Moore reaches his Jag, he finds another unsavory looking fellow sitting on the hood of his car.

"If you're looking to buy that car it's not for sale," said Moore.

"I'm not into buyin', I'm into takin'," said the taller man, now standing.

"Oh, my mistake, I thought you were a fuckin' car broker."

Before the rude guy counters Moore's reply, they're joined by the guy from across the street.

"What's this a frigging party?" said Agent Moore.

"You're coming with us, little man, we need to talk to you," said the much taller man from across the street as he nudges Agent Moore with whatever was inside his coat pocket. Moore plays along as the two men lead him down another block and shove him into an alley.

"Okay, Lil'-man," says the guy who's not so tall, "if you wanna date Crystal you got to pay us first."

"What-the...I assumed she was working independent?"

"Well, she ain't and this is how it works boy. That number she gave you is my phone. So when you use it, then you become my liability."

"Is that so?"

"Yeah, an in the meantime," said the shorter guy poking his index finger in Agent Moore's chest, "you owe me another hundred because you only paid up for half an hour and you went ten minutes overtime."

"Oh, I see, it's a fuckin' late fee that you're after."

The short pimp doing all the talking turns to give a wide grin to his partner, "Yeah, somethin' like that." His partner laughs heartily along with him but when they return their focus back to Agent Moore, he's holding a chrome .357 magnum in his left hand and it's aimed at their heads.

"Whoa-whoa! My bad, lil-shawty. We businessmen, brah. We ain't trying to jack you or nothing."

"Oh, so now I'm your brother, huh? Empty out them pockets you fuck-face motha' fucka's. Now!"

Agent Moore flips out his badge and holds it high so they can see it. The two men fumble through their pockets and out comes cell phones, two thick wads of cash, a pair of dice, key rings, five wallets and a .38 revolver. Moore had them turn and face the wall as he searches through the wallets to find out who they really are. He stuffs almost everything in his own pockets but he leaves behind two of the wallets and one wad of cash.

"You two dickheads can turn around now. But if I ever see you fuck-faces in the downtown area again, I'll have you thrown in jail for the next five years."

The two hustlers look dumbfounded, but with that said - Agent Moore spins on his heels and splits.

* * *

"Robbie, where in the world did that Agent Moore go to? It's already two o'clock and my stomach is growling at me."

"Have you forgot, there's food in the vending machine and it's free?"

"No way! I'm not messing with that generic yuk."

"Well, we could've stepped out for lunch an hour ago, but no, you're working this case like we're in some kind of a marathon."

"Well, it's not my fault Agent Shawty left us with a ton of film to wade through."

"That may be true, Doctor Ashley Watson but this Sherlock is hungry too. You make the choice, cuz we're in walking distance of Tony Roma's, the Pizzaria, or the Sicilian Deli that's two doors down."

"Gosh, Robbie, you make it sound like we're in a neighborhood that's run by the mob. The Pizzaria is fine, besides, it feels like ninety degrees in here. I could use a cold pitcher of beer."

Within minutes Rob and Ashley were chugging down their second glass of beer when the Canadian bacon pizza arrived. Rob slammed his empty beer goblet on the table then belched, and Ashley followed with a series of mini-burps while doodling her figures on the backside of a napkin.

"What'cha' doing, Kitten?"

"Huh?"

"The napkin," said Rob pointing.

"I'll answer your question just give me a sec." Ashley burps again. "Okay, I feel much better now," she giggles then continues. "The first piece of surveillance film we watched was on what was believed to be the morning of the diamond heist, right?"

"Yeah, as far as we could tell, someone who looks to be female hides herself in the cooler and during the wee hours of the morning, she creeps into the storage room with two black gym bags and comes out in less than an hour with the same two bags. Then she ducks into the shipping and receiving area and exits through the back door which sets off an alarm."

"Right, but the second film show apparently what seems like the same person coming out of the storage room and hiding something in different products on aisles three, five, six, and nine."

"It doesn't make sense?" clamors Rob.

"I'm baffled too, but if she hid diamonds in the products, why didn't she come back and get them? Or better yet, why didn't she just take all the diamonds out the first night she went in?"

"I don't know, but we mustn't overlook the fact that she also took a half million dollars in cash, which the public knows nothing about."

"Yeah, but we're still missing something. This still smells like an inside job when we consider the fact that only two Patel family members knew that the diamonds and cash were kept in the fabric store's basement."

"Yep, and that's why we've been hired, silly. Because the insurance company thinks it's an inside job and we've been hired by the Patels to prove it's not. If nobody gets reimbursed by the insurance company then nothing gets replaced."

"Okay, Sherlock Rob, but what puzzles me is the key. How did this burglar person who isn't a Patel nor an employee get hold of a key to the storage room in the first place, when there was supposed to be only 'one' key?"

"Well, we'll have to figure that one out once we take a look at more film. We may have to go back through several weeks of film to find that answer, though."

"Yuk! That doesn't sound like much fun," cried Ashley.

"It doesn't matter, because if we find something, fun or not, we're still getting paid."

* * *

Virgin Islands

Cat and I got bored for the Bahamas. Bobbie Ray still hadn't gotten all our money to us but we had enough to go wherever we wanted. After ten weeks, Ray paid us another visit. Cat and I tried to explain to him about the diamond heist and the details of our dilemma.

"I want my old life back, Ray."

"Me too!" shouts Cat. "We're tired of acting like were some wealthy folks playing tourist. I miss my Caddy!"

"And I miss Mugsy," I added, standing up with my hands on my hips like I was Wonder Woman.

"I've heard all of that from you two once before," replied Ray with a smirk, "but based on what you're telling me... Well, you can't go back to the States. Especially now, right?"

"No way!" I said.

"Yes-way! It's just common sense. Not only do you two have some mystery mobsters looking for you, but you're bound to have a team of investigators looking for you as well."

"Even if we're on film they can't implicate us, because all they seen us do was some shoppin'," argues Cat.

"Read my lips, ya'll two knuckle-headed crazy-ass women; them surveillance cameras are exactly what's gonna get the two of you caught up, because although the investigators may not be able to pin a thing on you, they'll want to question you regardless. So, once again, I'm suggesting that you shouldn't be lounging in any one area too long and it would be better for you to start thinking about starting a new life somewhere else."

Ray could see the bewilderment on our faces. Cat and I had to face the blunt naked truth, but a part of our nature wanted to believe that we would come out of this unscathed. We knew our only hope for returning to a normal life was to find that "Bitch" My Lai.

Ray kept talkin'... "Look, don't throw in the towel or give up on life just yet. You got goo-gobs of money at your fingertips right now, and there's a big wide ocean to explore."

"Sheee-it, if I do any more ex-plo-ratin' it will be on land!" cried Cat.

"Ya'll do it any way you like," countered Ray, "but in the meantime, I've got an emergency back in the States, so I'll hollar back in a couple weeks."

"Why the rush, Ray, what's goin on?"

"It's Houston. He's in the hospital. He's been shot."

"Shot!"

"Yeah, his dumb-ass gay friend put a bullet in 'em."

"What gay friend?" asked Cathy?"

"The little rich homosexual, Kenny Jackson. I guess Houston must of spurned him and the kid didn't take rejection so swell."

It was obvious to me by Ray's statement that he didn't know Kenny and Houston were tossing each other up. "Ray, are you sure the bullet was intended for Houston and not someone else?"

"Hell-if-I-know, Roxxy! But Houston should know betta' than to go fuckin' around with a skinny-legged nigga in tights."

* * *

CHAPTER TEN

Slick

A PIMP'S PROTECTION is very limited when a girl in his stable runs into trouble with a trick, especially if she's performing her trade in the trick's car or a rented room. Her pimp is usually kicking it with other pimps, or cutting up dope at another motel. Slick was no different. Even after several years had passed since I ran away fom his punk ass, he was still hustling barely legal chicks. You'd think he
would have elevated his game by now, but not Slick. He was old school and kinda' clever. His cop-and-blow style mentality was ingrained in him. He didn't keep watch over his chicks too closely unless he was unsure of their loyalty. If the chick didn't generate enough income or complained too much about the work, Slick wouldn't hesitate to dump her ass on some interstate highway without prior notice. That's because he wasn't into using the traditional coat hanger beatings or cigarette burns to keep a ho' in line. He didn't have time for that. It was cop-and-blow with him. If the chick fucked up one too many times she had to go, because there was plenty of other girls to choose from, and catching a fresh ho' and breaking her in was much more fun than spending time in jail for beatin' one down. So, if the chick got fucked over by a trick, he shrugged it off as one of the breaks of doing business.

Slick was the one who nicknamed me 'Candy Cane'. Part of his reason for choosing that name was due to my fiery red hair and freckled skin, but he also said I was the first girl he'd ever met that didn't need no training on how to suck a dick. I guess it never fazed me cuz despite his fake-ass compliment, I ran from him and never looked back.

After doing three years in jail for rolling johns, Slick went right back on the circuit again. For a couple years he ran prostitutes from Vancouver, Portland, San Francisco to Las Vegas, three to four weeks in one place then moved on to another city. His script was simple, have each girl stake out a location on the side of the road. They could wave at traffic or pretend to hitchhike. It didn't much matter to Slick. They could use whatever method they chose as long as it generated a good capital gain. He trained his girls to find out how much a trick was willing to spend, make them show the money, and by all means get the money first before getting started. Most of his girls were teenagers, 18 and up with a record, a runaway from home, or just running from another pimp. Occasionally, chicks he worked with came up missing, but he didn't have to worry about none of that until he ran into My Lai Smith.

Turns out that My Lai was not dead. She had been laying low in the desert town of Lebec, about twenty miles south of Bakersfield, right off Interstate 5. She had leased a home that was built underground to protect her from the harsh desert heat, which during peak summer season, averaged one-hundred-and-ten degrees. Still driving a Jeep Cherokee, she stopped in town for lunch and to pick up a few supplies. The fact that she ended up eating at a restaurant in a seat that was across the aisle from Slick and his chick, was possibly the worst thing that happen to him that day.

He was high on something and had slapped the girl, Melody, right in front of the patrons several times, just after the waitress brought over their order. Although Melody's cheeks were beet red from the back-handed strikes, the girl remained silent and never cried out.

"Lazy-ass cracker bitch!" scolded Slick. "You think this shit grows on trees?"

He was shaking a fist of twenties in her face. His own face was puffy and his eyes were blood-shot red from too much booze and sun. His short-hair was freshly cut, and his deep waves were dipping in a 360-degree circle.

Melody attempted to re-light her cigarette and ignore Slick's rant, but he wasn't having it. He slapped the cigarette from her lips before she had a chance to flick her Bic lighter, and that's when My Lai got up from her seat and walked up to the feuding couple's table. My Lai made the hooker scoot over and took the seat facing Slick.

My Lai had gained a few pounds. Wearing an extra-large white T-shirt with the sleeves cut off, she had it tucked inside army-fatigues. She wore a shiny pair of black Desert Storm boots and a hat like Pharrel wore when he sang that song "Happy". Her beefed-up arms were bronze. She looked like a female Billy Jack.

"What the fuck do you want, woman!" snorted Slick.

"She no talk. So I talk for her, big boy."

"Boy! Who you callin' 'boy', woman!"

"I don't see no man, so I call it like I see it," spat My Lai.

By now all the patrons had stopped eating and drinking and with frozen faces, stared directly at the trio.

Slick gave a cruel smile and leered at My Lai. He was oblivious to the people sitting around him. Suddenly, his fist flashed across the table as he attempted to snatch My Lai by the collar and that was his mistake. In an instant, everything went red, then yellow when My Lai made a lightening quick military move. In what seemed to onlookers as one single motion, My Lai caught Slick's thumb, twisted his forearm, and yanked his shoulder out of socket. Then she rose from her seat still twisting and never letting go. She had his elbow locked like she was trying to break it.

Slick, holding his breath refused to cry out, but he held the palm of his free hand up as he grimaced in pain.

When My Lai rose from her seat, Melody bolted and ran out the restaurant's side door. Then My Lai released her hold on him and backed away, never taking her eyes from his cold twisted stare.

If he was embarrassed, he didn't show it. When the waitress showed up and timidly handed him his bill, Slick reached into his top shirt pocket and slapped two twenties on the table and shouted, "Imma get you, bitch! Just wait—you steroid-ass robotic-lookin' mutha- fucka'."

With that said, he stomped his way to his vehicle and slammed the door as My Lai kept watch from the restaurant's plate glass window.

Slick's ride was a Mercedes Benz G-class SUV. The body was money-green and so was the interior. He had the windows murdered out, all blackened, with white powder coated rims. His tires screeched from the parking lot in search of Melody, the hooker who'd just run off.

If you've never lived in the desert, well let me tell you, it ain't nothing nice. The heat can envelope you like a hot wet blanket or it can swat you like you's a lazy-ass fly. When I lived in the desert I never went outside unless it was to get in and out of someone's car. The home I lived in couldn't afford an air conditioner, so we had a swamp cooler, a machine that blows cool air over a giant sponge that's soaked in water. It would cause the temperature in any room to lower. So when it's a hundred degrees outside, it's only about eighty-five degrees in the house. I know it doesn't sound like much help but believe me, it made a big difference.

Anyway, My Lai was living underground which was a whole lot cooler than dwellings above ground. Her home was marked by a weather vane on top of a sloping ground level roof line. Other than the skimpy row of twenty foot tall desert pines that surrounded a big vegetable garden, there were flowers but not too many. The trees and garden were the main indicator that the home was actually hidden there.

When Melody streaked from the restaurant, she caught a ride with a woman who was headed into the heart of downtown. She had the lady drop her off at the Greyhound station and she took the first bus that was headed north on Interstate 5. Melody didn't allow the bus to travel far. She pulled on the cord at the first railway stop. It was at that point she realized the little money she had would only get her to Bakersfield, and Slick would find her quick because he'd grown up there and knew everybody in town. As she sat at the bus stop bench contemplating her next move, a Jeep pulled up and honked. Cautiously approaching, she recognized My Lai.

"Where you goin'?" asked My Lai after rolling down the passenger side window.

"Nowhere in particular. I guess I'm just waiting for a pimp to show up."

"No you're not," My Lai said, as she swung the door open, "Get in."

They talked very little during the four mile drive down Center, a dusty desert road. My Lai finally pulled into her private oasis and cut the engine.

"Okay, Melody, you're welcome to chill out with me until we can decide what your next move should be. Maybe it will give you time to get your head straight because I can tell you're not accustomed to life in the desert. Where are you from?"

Melody, without a hint of hesitation in her voice, decided to lie, "I'm from South San Francisco, Daly City to be exact."

"I know the place," replies My Lai, "been there a couple times myself." My Lai was checking out Melody who didn't look a day beyond eighteen. She was a pretty Portuguese brunette with brown eyes that displayed way too much mascara. Her eyebrows were thick and perfectly shaped, and she had pock marked dimpled cheeks. Her skin had an orange tint, burnt by the scorching sun. She wore a white cotton twill ball cap, a florescent green halter top that didn't quite reach her navel. Her Wrangler Jeans were white, tennis shoes were plaid, a shade of pink, purple and blue. She carried a stretched out knitted purse that was jammed packed with everything she owned.

Upon entering the underground home, Melody was amazed by the spaciousness and coolness of the room. It was equipped with most of the amenities found in a home above ground. There was a wood burning stove, a refrigerator and freezer, and plenty of lighting all powered by several portable generators. Among the furnishings were two couches, a table, cabinets, and a portable toilet and shower stall. Everything was orderly and neat, and the air was surprisingly fresh, not musty nor stale.

"Both of my couches fold out into beds," explained My Lai. "You can place your things on that one over there," she indicated by pointing to the couch that was next to the freezer. "Help yourself to anything in the fridge that suits your appetite. There's fresh fruit and vegetables in the pantry as well. I spend a lot of my spare time in the garden. You're welcome to join me. There's a well and a concrete tub under a shed. You can wash clothes there or bathe if you like. I normally only drive into town on weekends, usually to do some shopping or occasionally take in a movie. You can tag along if you want to."

Melody wasn't in a very talkative mood for the first few days. My Lai wasn't one to push. She figured the girl would open up to her in time.

When their first weekend together arrived, Melody chose not to go into town. No less than twenty minutes had gone by when she realized she just smoked her last cigarette, so she began a frantic search throughout the house. My Lai was a hoarder, so there were a lot of places to pack some smokes. Melody was careful to put back everything the exact way she found them, but after an hour she gave up. My Lai was a heavy smoker but there was no stash of cigarettes or butts in an ashtray to be found. Melody surmised that the cigarettes were kept somewhere inside My Lai's Jeep.

Now totally frustrated, she slammed a pail against the siding of the freezer and a panel snapped open. Rushing over to fix it, she tried to snap it shut but couldn't get it to slip back into place. She had no real mechanical skills, but after closer examination she realized there was a plastic red cooler that filled some type of hidden storage space. Curious, she pulled the cooler chest out, unsnapped the lid, and then her hands flew up to her mouth..."Oh-my-God, oh-my-God, oh-my-God," she said aloud. It was as though she were hyperventilating. Staring back at her were bundles of twenties, fifties and hundred dollar bills shrink-wrapped in plastic.

Melody panicked. She thought she heard the crunch of gravel and a car engine rumble. She shut the cooler's lid, shoved it back in its hiding place, and ran out the door. After a quick search, no auto nor person was found, so she rushed back inside and used the extra security bolt to double lock the door.

The first layer was the money, and underneath she found the stones. There were hundreds of them in large zip-lock baggies, at least four times bigger than the average sandwich bag. Each bag contained a different color, white, yellow, blue, brown, and red gems. At first glance, Melody thought they were a jeweler's glass beads, but there were no holes in the centers so they had to be stones. She was attracted to the ruby reds so she opened a baggie and poured a few in her hand then held them up to the light. They dazzled, shining in every direction. Her mind raced. My Lai had been gone for more than a couple hours she thought. Melody wasn't quite sure, because she'd lost track of time. She hurried. She retrieved a brown handkerchief and three pill receptacles from her purse. She dumped out the medication and filled the tiny retainers with jewels and stashed them in the bottom of her purse.

* * *

By the time My Lai returned, Melody had tidied up the house and was out under the shed washing the few clothes she had. She stopped what she was doing to help My Lai carry some bags of groceries inside.

"I'm good," said My Lai, after tossing Melody a shopping bag. "Here, that's for you."

"Huh?"

My Lai went inside the house with her groceries and Melody trailed behind. Melody's bag held a fresh pair of sandals, a carton of cigarettes, and a pair of designer sun glasses.

"Wow, thanks, Me Lie!" her face was now a flush pink because she was a little embarrassed, "You must of read my mind," she giggled.

My Lai lit a cigarette and begins a smile at the right corner of her mouth. Blowing a stream of smoke through the other she said, "Tomorrow, I'm going to Bakersfield to take in a movie. Want to come?"

"Yeah, I think I'll take you up on that," said Melody while opening a fresh pack of her own smokes and returning a smile.

The following afternoon, they stuck to their plans and took a drive up to one of Bakersfield's downtown tri-cinemas. There were six movies showing. The girls made their selections and My Lai purchased the tickets, but before going in Melody wanted to make a quick trip to a next door market.

"You go ahead, Mel," said My Lai. "I'll be in the third row, front-left of the center aisle."

"Okay, this won't take me but a minute. If you have time, grab me a box of popcorn."

My Lai enters the theater while Melody zipped around the corner. She bypassed the market and heads for a nearby jewelry store but it was closed. She rambled back towards the theater and noticed a pawn shop that's open directly across from the theater. Upon entering, she finds that the place is not large and it's got a lone customer doing business at the far end of the counter. She retreats to the opposite end and digs deep inside her purse when an attendant sneaks up on her and clears his throat.

"Is there something special you're looking for?"

Slightly startled, Melody replies, "Yeah, just a sec." She finally locates one of the containers, pops the cap and rolls a fat blue gem stone onto the counter. It's a two and one half carat diamond.

The attendant's name tag reads "Wookie". Wookie quickly picks up the stone and flips it in his palm.

"What will you give me for that?" asked Melody."

"If it's costume jewelry, not much," assured the attendant with a smirk. Nevertheless, Wookie is slightly puzzled because the stone has got plenty of heft and sparkle. It could be the real deal. He reaches under the counter and pulls out an eyepiece, a magnifying lens and begins his inspection of the stone, "I'll give you a hundred dollars for this ma'am. You got any more?"

Melody returns the smirk and thrust her right palm up, almost jamming it into Wookie's face, "Give it back!" she barks. "I'll take my business elsewhere."

Finishing with the previous customer, the owner of the shop comes over to lend a hand. He's an older guy with a gruffy white beard. He's wearing a brown bow tie, a white shirt, and a frayed olive colored suit.

He's a lot shorter than Wookie, five-foot-six, same height as Melody. He stares into her dark brown eyes, "Hello, madam. May I have a look?"

Melody hands the old man the stone and watches him closely as he goes through his little ritual of searching his vest pocket for his own personal eyepiece, fumbling around for a second, then finally inspecting the stone. He scrapes it against a pane of glass. For a brief moment everyone seems to be holding their breath, realizing that only a real diamond can cut through glass.

"I'll give you five hundred cash," announces the old man.

"No, thanks," replies Melody reaching for the blue rock once again.

"Hmmm..." contemplates the old man pulling at his whiskers, "show me five more like this one and I'll give you four thousand for the set."

Melody rolls twelve diamonds of various colors onto the counter. In less than ten minutes she arrives at the cinema with ten thousand dollars stuffed inside her Wrangler pockets and takes the seat next to My Lai. My Lai hands her a box of popcorn and a Big Gulp Seven-up.

* * *

Back at the pawn shop, Wookie grumbled, "That was an awfully generous transaction, boss."

"No, not really," countered his boss. "I gave her a quarter of what they are actually worth."

"You're kiddin'!"

"No, I'm not. I'm just hoping she's got a lot more of those puppies and when she comes back, we'll work her like she's a prime rib steak."

"Ha, that's if she comes back."

Later that night, Wookie made a phone call, "Hey Slick!"

"Yeah, what up, homie?"

"Guess what...one of your chicks came by the shop today."

"Who?"

"You know, the one that ran off."

"Melody?"

"Yeah, that one."

"Okay, tell me something I should know."

"Well, she cashed in some fat-ass rocks in exchange for ten grand."

"Ten grand! Where in the fuck that bitch get a grip like that?"

"How in the fuck am I supposed to know...but look, I made a few calls and it seems she's been seen hanging out with that Asian chick that you had a run-in with awhile back."

"You don't say. You know how to find her?"

"The Asian chick?"

"Yeah."

"No, but I'll get back at you when I do."

"Okay, but do it soon, 'cause Melody owes me big time. And don't worry, I got your back. When I come up, so will you, and you can take that to the bank, fool."

"Okay, Slick Brah', I feel ya!"

* * *

Melody couldn't believe her good fortune. She had a hard time sleeping that night because the realization that she was sleeping next to a treasure chest was creating one insane dream followed by another. After getting out of bed to have a smoke for the third time, she knew there was no other choice but to make up an excuse to leave without arousing My Lai's suspicions. So while in town earlier that evening, she bought herself a disposable cell phone and made a call to San Jose.

"Hello, Crystal?"

"Melody, you lame-ass hefa'. What you callin' a bitch so early for? I ain't heard from you in a month of Sundays. I thought you was dead, girlfriend."

"Crystal, don't be mad at me. I ran into some trouble and I had to get away for a while. But-hey, that 'G' I owe you...I got it, plus some more, but I need a little help."

"Where are you, hefa'?"

"I'm living at 1040 Center Road, in this spot outside of Lebec."

"Lebec? Where in the fuck is that?"

"It's a little town just south of Bakersfield."

"Melody, you know I ain't got no wheels. Can't you just take a Greyhound up this way?"

"Greyhound won't work for us this time. We need some screaming wheels with some heat under the hood, if you know what I'm saying."

Crystal knew by Melody's tone that she had come into something big and whatever it was it probably involved a whole lot of money. She remembered the last time Melody ran off with a hundred grand that she found in one of her trick's briefcases, so it wasn't the first time Crystal had come to her rescue. Lucky for the pair of prostitutes, the trick was an accountant who ended up doing time for an embezzlement scheme, and the hundred grand that Melody ripped him off for was only five percent of what he'd stolen from the firm he worked for.

"Okay, bitch, I'mma see what I can do. Give me a number and I'll hollar back as soon as I hook somethin' up."

It was a week before Crystal actually made that callback. In the meantime, My Lai had begun to take a serious interest in helping out Melody. The girl wasn't a dope addict and she wasn't afraid of hard work. When My Lai was away on business, Melody was keeping up on the garden work all by herself. My Lai figured if she taught her a few survival skills it might help change Melody's outlook on life or at least stop her from giving her hard earned money over to a pimp. My Lai began giving her lessons on hand-to-hand combat, the basics of weaponry, and how to use a gun. She also gave her wages for helping out in the garden and around the home.

When Melody finally got the call back from Crystal, Melody was having second thoughts about following through with her plan to rip My Lai off.

"You silly, bitch!" wailed Crystal. "I went through a lot of trouble to put this move down, so you betta' be ready to jet when I come by."

"Just chill a minute, mighty mouth. We're gonna do this, okay. But first we've got to be extra careful because this chick is ex-military and if we leave a trail she'll hunt us down."

Melody hadn't fully decided whether she wanted to clean My Lai out or just liberate a portion of her treasure. She had enough sense to figure that My Lai's stash of money and gems had possibly been ripped off from someone else and that My Lai was laying low until it was safe to move or flip the merchandise.

Melody thought that it might be wise to leave the money untouched. There were twenty bags of gem stones and there appeared to be a couple thousand diamonds in each bag. Melody liked the red diamonds, but if she took all the reds My Lai would be instantly alerted, and selling only red would leave a trail. Melody noticed that some bags were marked "FAKES", and it caused her to wonder if all the diamonds not marked were real. She meticulously replaced everything back as though nothing had ever been touched.

*   *   *

During the second week of August, the Mojave's desert heat averaged a 110° degrees. On a Thursday evening My Lai informed Melody that she would be taking a short trip down-south Friday morning and that she wouldn't return until Saturday afternoon. When Friday arrived, My Lai sent Melody out to pick a crop of vegetables and fruits that she would be taking on her trip. While Melody was doing the chores, My Lai slid the home's front door dead-bolt in place and checked on her stash. She removed a stack of twenties and two bags of gems and stuffed them in a carry case on wheels. Next, she shut the red cooler chest and shoved it under the freezer when she noticed two red diamonds lying in the crack of the concrete floor.

With a Swiss Army knife, she pried them loose and examined the stones. She was always careful whenever she handled the gems and didn't recall ever removing any loose stones unless she was at her work table where she laid out a white sheet. In an instant, her mind raced and several unlikely scenarios crossed her mind, but she pushed them aside because she couldn't afford to keep the people waiting that she was going out of town to see.

* * *

Slick couldn't afford to waste time. He was an opportunist and in this case he had to be patient and wait for the opportunity to present itself. He'd set up a spyglass on a desert bluff about a quarter mile out from My Lai's oasis. It was from his hide-away that he observed the two women working the garden on a daily basis. He was amused when My Lai went through martial art drills as well as her attempts at teaching Melody how to shoot down a target from fifty, then, a hundred feet. Slick had just finished setting up his watch camp at 10:00 a.m. when he saw My Lai start up her jeep and hightail it down the desert road. He smiled to himself, and it occurred to him that sometimes it's better to let a woman run, and when you catch up to her you keep the fight clean — but the sex extra dirty. Well, the opportunity had presented itself and Slick was more than ready to checkmate Melody and put a crimp in My Lai's game.

Within only minutes of My Lai's departure, another vehicle arrived and there was a black chick driving. Slick watched as she climbed out of a classic grey 1974 Plymouth Road Runner, with a 318 under the hood, a three speed shift on the floor, and glass packs on the muffler. Slick was too far away to recognize the chick's face, but her strut looked vaguely familiar. So he decided to make his move just as the two girls disappeared inside the home.

Stepping down into the house, Crystal grabs a handful of Melody's ass, "Oooouhh, you been eatin' good up in here, bitch! That dyke been feedin' you sweet potatoes from her garden?...teh-he-hee."

Melody doesn't turn around but she quickly slaps Crystal's hand away, "Get out my business, Crystal, and quit it. Me Lie ain't no dyke and I don't bump pussy. That's your department."

"Ex-cuuuuse me. Why you getting' all huffy with me, like you worried about the earth moving closer to the sun or something?"

"Fuuuk-you! Silly be-atch, besides, I thought you said you'd be driving a Jaguar XJ8. What happened, your little agent boyfriend change his mind about you?"

"Humph, I got that little freak wrapped around my pinky toe. He loaned me a car from his private collection an--"

"THUMP-Thump-Thump!"

"Who's that?" yelped Crystal, her hazel eyes looming.

Melody doesn't hesitate. She reached around her back, pulled out My Lai's Glock 17 and says, "Who is it!"

"U.S. Postal," said the voice, "I have a package for Me Lie Smith."

"Just leave it by the door. I'll see to it that she gets it."

"Sorry, ma'am, I can't do that, unless I get a signature on the invoice slip."

Melody brings her left index finger to her lips, and directs Crystal to take cover as she creeps toward the front door, the only entrance to the house. The door automatically locks when it closes, so whomever is outside, can't get in.

Slick, now suffering from impatience, rattles the door knob, and Melody fires two quick shots. The gun blasts leave splintered holes through the door as gun smoke fills the room. Then there's Creep Show dead silence as the girls hold their positon. After a few minutes have passed, they hear the slow crunch of gravel and a vehicle driving off. Melody cautiously approaches the door with Crystal crouching behind her.

"What the fuck!" screeched Crystal. "Girlfriend, you done conned my ass into coming out here in these boondocks just so I can get my cap peeled! No-you-did-ent!"

"Calm down, Sista' Sledge...let me show you something before you turn Hila Monster on me."

Melody walks over to the freezer, kneels, and removes the panel.

Crystal looks around the room with panic stricken eyes before she joins Melody as they muscle the red chest from underneath the freezer.

* * *

Slick cursed to himself for moving in on his prey too quickly. He thought of three better ways he could have gone about it but it was too late to concern himself with "What If's"... Due to the fact that there were no windows in the underground house to peek from, the girls hadn't seen him nor had they recognized his voice. Slick retreated to his hideaway, and using his cell phone, he made a call.

"Hey, Wookie, it's me, Slick! We gon' have to go to plan 'B'. I see them leaving now."

"Them?" said Wookie.

"Yeah, there's two of them, Melody and a hooker named Crystal. I recognized the bitch by the way she walk. They're driving a seventy-four Road Runner. It's grey. It's a raggedy lookin' mutha' fucka but it's got a hemi, so beware cause it's fast. You park yourself at Pacheco Point just like we talked about, a mile pass Wheeler's Ridge. We'll sandwich them in, then run 'em off the road."

"You forgettin' there's steep canyons on both sides of that part of the highway?"

"Fucken-eh, buddy, accidents are just waitin' to happen. You know what I'm sayin?"

* * *

When My Lai pulled into the circular driveway mansion at Santa Clarita, an odd feeling came over her. It was just a gut feeling that something at home had been overlooked. After completing the business at hand, she cancelled her reservations at a restaurant and the overnight hotel. She boomeranged her way back to her oasis in the desert. After bypassing the town of Lebac, she went off-road and blazed a trail to the rear of her home.

Hoisting a Remington twelve gauge over her left shoulder, she kicked her front door open. The smell of cordite, from the Glock that Melody fired was still in the air. The panel from the freezer was askew and a shrink-wrapped stack of one hundred dollar bills lay on the cement floor alongside two zip lock bags of diamonds. My Lai crouched by the remains of her loot and took a deep breath. She reasoned that although Melody did a scandalous thing, she still had heart. My Lai trusted the bitch even when her gut told her otherwise. She should have at least locked-down her place and put the bitch out when she discovered those red diamonds out of place.

My Lai took a quick inventory of her space and noticed an off-brand cigarette butt with a lipstick print in the ashtray. Instantly, she knew that some female had either robbed or assisted with the rip-off.

My Lai took a trip back to her Jeep and returned with a laptop. She hooked it up to a hidden cable which led to a camera that was mounted on her roof and camouflaged by the weather vane. From a stream of video footage she had all the info she would need to track the scum who had stolen her gems.

Outside she found two separate trails, one solo and a pair going in an opposite direction. There were tire tracks but only one of them took the normal route to the roadway. My Lai went back inside and dug out a Smith & Wesson .44 Magnum and some extra ammunition. When she hit the freeway pavement, she was headed north on Interstate 5.

*   *   *

Slick and Wookie were cut from a similar mold. Like salt and pepper they were a good combo. Pinched together or sifted apart, they lived for the thrill of seeking fortune, women, and cars. Slick-slim, brown-eyed and brown skinned, Wookie-slightly taller, light-complexion, with green eyes. Slick-dashing, intelligent and reserved, Wookie-flamboyant, cunning and versatile.

The California Aqueduct intertwines and often runs parallel to Interstate 5, a four-lane stretch of interstate. There's a few kinks and swerves, but no hellacious curves, just a lot of pickup trucks and slow moving semi's. There are a slew of intricate canyons, going North towards Bakersfield, near the Interstate 99 merge, and for that reason it's not a place to pretend you're on a — German autobahn or NASCAR sprint circuit. Crystal didn't have any respect for the interstate's trepidation. She was hot dogging the Road Runner like a qualifying run at a Laguna Seca speedway. With Melody bravely strapped like a crash test dummy in the passenger seat, they came up on Wookie's rear and screamed past him like a supersonic missile while he was dialing up chill-out tunes from his Caddy's digital console. The girls left him dodging traffic through a caravan of semi's and a stream of SUV's.

When Slick 's money green Mercedes caught up to Wookie's CTS, the dubious pair had no choice but to get on with the chase. Yet their attempts at overtaking the hookers would soon be thwarted by two Highway Patrolmen who were lurking in the shadows. The speeding automobiles hurling through traffic at break-neck speeds were instant attention getters, and the CHP's were now in hot pursuit.

*   *   *

CHAPTER ELEVEN

Benji

THIS RUNNIN' GAME, island hopping, and pretending we rich had played out for Cat and I. Besides, after our offshore accounts tapered off at six point five million, somehow, Bobbie Ray's folks ran into a situation. Some forensic government computer experts went through somebody's files and e-mails. Next, warrants were obtained for storage units, property and our money flow just froze. For the moment Cat and I are satisfied with what we have, so we decide to cut our losses and take our chances returning to the South Bay.

* * *

A thread of light appeared under a crevice where floor meets door. Agent Moore didn't expect to find the chat room occupied at 9:00 p.m. He keyed the door, stepped inside, and took a look around. The furniture and office decor had been rearranged. The lights were left on but the room was empty of personnel until Rob and Ashley came barging through the unlocked door.

"It's just me, folks. No need to get all excited," squawked Agent Moore.

"Where in the world have you been," cried Ashley, her light blue eyes looming large as if she had been drinking huge cups of coffee all day.

Agent Moore didn't bother to reply. He was looking up at the wall monitor as the green florescence light cast an eerie reflection on his face, exposing layers of wrinkles around his eyes. His lofty attitude annoyed Ashley.

"By the way, Mr. Shawty, I saw you at the shopping mall with that hooker, that doppledangler lookin' chick."

"Is that so," replied Agent Moore as if he didn't care. "Well, it seems someone had nothing better to do than rearrange the furnishings while I was gone."

"Yeah, Ashley moved the vending machines a couple feet," said Rob with a chuckle, trying to break the ice in the room. His attempt didn't work and Ashley threw a shitty fit.

"Kiss my grits, Agent Shawty, cuz I'm feeling kinda nuclear right now and you don't want me to go bananas on you--"

"Oh, do forgive me, Madam Ashley, I know I haven't been keeping the two of you informed like I promised, but sometimes I break my own rules. I'm a grown man and I can do whatever the hell I want," replied Moore raising his tone an octive. He looks back at Ashley with a funny stare and a plastic smile. He's arrogant, the kind of guy that would prefer to slap a maitre d' and order him to find a seat rather than make a reservation.

"Robbie, don't light nothin' around me cuz I just might explode!" erupts Ashley. "You ain't no shot caller from Washington DC, you--"

"Enough you two!", pleads Rob. "Can we get serious for just a minute?"

"No way, cuz he's all up in here!" Ashley spreads a palm to her face and gets up in Moore's grill.

"And you're a snide bitch," hissed Moore.

"That's a friggin' lie!" howls Ashley.

"That's it!," yells Rob as he glares at Ashley.

"Well, excuuuse me," replied Ashley trading looks, "but those chocolate chip cookies in that machine are calling me." She waddled away with her pony tail swishing.

Finally, the arguing stopped and the three agents got down to business and compared notes.

"The film footage reveals there's other operatives. Women who's identities were unknown at first," said Rob, "until Ashley and I ran into a little luck. We checked the locksmiths in the area and a vendor recognized a picture of the Asian chick that he remembers doing business with on several occasions. He said her name is My Lai. She's got a sand paper face and multiple piercings on her left ear. He didn't know exactly what kind of work she did, but on one visit she wore a uniform and a holstered side arm. The locksmith was a Navy Vet and said her mannerisms reminded him of shore patrol personnel, and that each time she came in, she was driving a brown and beige Jeep."

As soon as Rob finished, Ashley cuts in without giving Agent Moore a chance to respond, "I also took time to check out the storage room a little more thoroughly, Shawty, and found a raincoat. Apparently it belonged to no one who works here. There were a couple strands of hair stuck to the collar and I had them tested for DNA. A person by the name of Roxanne Blackwell came up as a match. Apparently her and her girlfriend, Cathy Wilson, which may be one of the other females we got on film, are both under an FBI investigation for some sort of banking fraud down in Sunnyvale. I spoke to the FEDs and they seemed to have lost track of both Wilson and Blackwell. They suspect they may have moved outside the U.S."

Agent Moore gave Ashley a 'cat just ate the canary' smile and preens in the office mirror like he's Prince or Morris Day. Ashley gawks awaiting his reply.

"So you're thinking that these girls are the culprits responsible for helping set up the diamond heist and they're laying low until they find a fence to do business with and split the profits?"

"That's exactly what we're thinking," replied Rob. "But since the FBI had nothing solid to pin on them, they contend that the diamond heist is not their case unless Etna Insurance invites them in. But we figure if these women were involved in the diamond heist, then they're bound to return to the South Bay and cash in on the rest of their holdings."

"You don't say," said Agent Moore. "Once again, I'm two steps ahead of you private dicks! The hooker I've been hanging out with--"

"Oh, you mean the one with the funny lookin' tits?" blurts Ashley.

"Fuuucck you!" crows Agent Moore. "Yeah, that one," he rallies with a smirk. "And she's not as dingy as she looks, Madam Ashley. It just so happens that with her assistance I was able to find Blackwell's penthouse location. I bet the FBI didn't share that tidbit with you." Both Rob and Ashley frown. "Yeah, that's right," continues Moore,
"and I also interviewed the neighbors that are taking care of Miss. Blackwell's pit bull. And that friend of her's Wilson, she's got a vintage Cadillac in storage. The girls have been out of town for close to three months. They left no information on their destination nor did they indicate when they'd return, but everyone I spoke to was certain the women were coming back soon."

* * *

Benji Patel, the Drug Thrift Store pharmacist, was a handsome man with friendly grey eyes. His charming and cordial personality was a primary asset that kept preferred customers shopping at the variety store. However, his constant stream of carnal thoughts for the female patrons never ceased, despite having a near fatal stroke and being rushed to the hospital a few months ago. Still, the memory of what led up to that shameful event still haunts him. It happened when a woman hiding out in the storage room caught him in the middle of a mastabatory act. Eventually, it became evident that the mystery woman was the one responsible for stealing the diamonds from his
brother's vault. How had she known?... What happened to her? Would he ever see her again?...These were some of the recurring thoughts that

wouldn't go away. The diamonds and cash were the least of his concerns because his family was assured the insurance coverage would recoup all their losses. Nevertheless, the pharmacist had a more pressing matter to attend to. His son, Benji Junior, was in his third year of studies at U.C. Davis, for veterinary medicine when he was arrested for prowling and trespassing. Although Benji Senior hired a reputable criminal lawyer who had gotten the media to minimize the storied details, Benji Senior was deeply concerned for his son's future and well-being.

According to Benji Junior, his arrest was just a misunderstanding, at least that's the way his lawyer explained it to the media. Benji Junior was tall, dark, confident, and at the top of his class. He had no problem getting dates with girls, but the complaint came from a women's dorm. Like his father, Benji Junior had a kinky side, a side that classmates knew nothing about, because Junior was a peeping tom.

* * *

The caw of crows was the only thing that felt country along San Jose's South Monterey Road. Along this path, you'd find a stretch of used car lots, trailer parks, and flea bag motels intermingled with fruit stands displaying their summer's harvest — watermelons, cantaloupes, grapes, plums, and strawberries. It was a time of year for Silicon Valley's County Fair, carnivals, and the best time to visit a vineyard.

The only thing Benji Junior didn't like about the summer was that it didn't get dark until around 8:45 p.m. His idea of prime time entertainment was deciding on what area he'd prowl and which windows he'd peek through. He needed a building that provided plenty of shadowy shrubbery for cover. The flea bag motels down Monterey Road was one of his favorite locations, along with the hookers that paraded up and down the road from nine until midnight on most summer nights.

When Crystal and Melody came barreling into the city limits of San Jose, they held onto Agent Moore's Road Runner for several days. They got settled at the Shangra-La Lounge, a flea bag motel on Monterey Road. Benji Junior, for the last three nights, parked his car on a neighboring street. He used an alley to cross a fence bordering the twenty-four cottages at the Shangra-La Lounge. With only three feet of space between the cottage and the fence, Benji had to do his prowling in a very tight space.

Melody and Crystal were completely unaware that Benji's roving eyes had been invading their privacy. He observed the girls lounging in panties, bras and on one night he caught a glimpse of Crystal stepping out of the shower completely nude. Tonight he decided to stay longer hoping to catch them doing some raunchy sex.

When Benji reached his hiding place around 10:00 p.m., the girls were not home and the lights were turned off, so the cottage's interior was pitch black. Benji, dressed in black running gear, had no other choice but to wait patiently in the dark. After waiting close to an hour, Benji sprang from his post when a loud muffler from a muscle car pulled into the carport. Exiting the car was Melody and Crystal, strapped with packages in both arms. Melody keyed the cottage door and flicked the light switch on...

"Surprise!" cackled Slick, as he lay comfortably on a king sized water bed.

"Don't be bashful, come on in," said Wookie seated in a chair that was leaning against a window sill.

Crystal dropped her bags on the floor, "What ch'all doing in here? Are you hidin' out from the police?"

"Ask your girlfriend," answered Slick. "She knows what this is about."

"How did you find us?" moaned Melody, still holding onto her groceries.

"We been chasing you two tricks for a week!" snorted Slick. "You know you can't run from me, woman, cuz I knows everybody there is to know from San Diego to Vancouver and all points in between."

"Well, you found us, and their ain't nothing here for you so get ta steppin'." Melody dropped her bag of groceries, reached behind her back and flashed My Lai's Glock 17. She took aim directly at Slick 's head, "One...two--"

"Hold up, Sista'," protested Slick. "We didn't come up in here to get violent with ya'll."

He was trying to smooth talk as if he wasn't under any duress.

Wookie remained seated and calm. He never flinched.

"Don't test me, Slick," countered Melody. "I'm way past the flattery bullshit talk. I'm not your merchandise any more. Crystal and I have gone into business for ourselves."

"Yeah, that's right!" co-signs Crystal. "And if you ask me, you two should just beat it!"

"Nobody asked you a muthat fuckin' thing!" snapped Slick. "This here is a two-way conversation, woman. So I suggest you shut the fuck up or Wookie is going to see to it that you do."

"I ain't scared of no hooligan. You fuck with me and I'll bust a cap in his ass and your's too!" said Crystal, sounding serious.

Slick laughs laboriously and so does Wookie, but the laughter ends abruptly when Crystal reached down her boot and pulls out a pearl handled .25 caliber automatic pistol.

Wookie rears out of his seat and Crystal shoots... "BANG!" The bullet whistles past Wookie's left ear and crashes through the window. The crash of shattering glass is followed by a thud coming from somewhere outside.

"Dumb ass bitches!" shouts Slick. "Ya'll put them things away before somebody gets hurt."

But Wookie is looking through the gaping hole, "Hey, there's someone out there!"

Slick slides off the water bed and hops over to the window, "Son-of-a-bitch! Woman, you done kilt somebody."

Sprawled between the eight foot pine fence and the side of the cottage is Benji Patel Junior, bleeding from the left side of his skull. Melody and Crystal still have their guns aimed at the two men but the men ignore them.

"Who is that?" moans Slick.

"I don't know?" replies Wookie. "But whoever he is he was probably spying on us."

"Do you think he's dead?"

"Well, if he ain't he will be shortly. Let's get outta' here."

"No way! Not just yet," commands Melody.

Slick and Wookie turn to face the girls.

"I hate to be the bearer of bad news, but we're not staying where we're not welcomed. We'll be on our way."

The men take a few steps toward the door and Melody rushed to the window and views the body, "Wait, wait," urges Melody, "let's make a deal."

"What are you sayin'!" barks Crystal. "Is that guy really dead?"

"I don't know," replies Melody. "Look, fella's."

"WHAT!" the men shout back with a snarl.

"Shh! Keep your voices down. I'm offering you a proposition here. You help us get rid of the body and I'll make you rich," says Melody.

"Rich? Okay, so what's the deal?" probed Slick rubbing his hand under his chin.

"Crystal, get the stuff," Melody told her.

Crystal opens the door to the closet and pulls the string dangling from an overhead light bulb. She removes a panel from the closet's hardwood floor, reaches inside the hole and comes up with two bricks of hundred dollar bills shrink-wrapped in cellophane. She tosses one to Slick and the other to Wookie. Both men are grinning but suddenly there's a knock on the cottage door.

"Who is it?" said Melody.

"Open your door, Ms. Springer. I need to speak with you," said the man with a Middle Eastern accent.

"It's the manager," whispers Crystal. She closes the closet door and the men move over toward the window, their bodies blocking the shattered glass, while Melody timidly opens the front door.

"Sorry to disturb you, Miss. Springer, but your neighbor has filed a complaint about having heard arguing and a gunshot coming from your room." As the motel manager speaks, his bulbous eyes take inventory of the room and the faces of the people in it. He smells the cordite from the shot that's been fired.

Melody shakes her head from side to side and says, "No, the neighbor was mistaken. We heard it too, but it sounded like it came from the other side of that fence."

"Okay, so everything is fine here?" the manager asked.

Almost everyone nods their head simultaneously, "Yes, of course," insists Melody with a smile.

"Well, that is good, but I must warn you...the neighbor has called the police so it may be wise to leave now unless you're ready to answer a lot more questions. Oh yes, and don't forget to drop the room key in the box outside the office window."

* * *

Slick and Wookie tapped out the remaining glass in the window pane and muscled the body into the cottage. Wookie checked for a pulse but there was none, Benji appeared to be dead. Every feature in his face looked frozen. His mouth and eyes were wide open. The two men wrapped him in two bed sheets and stuffed him in the trunk of Wookie's Cadillac CTS, while the girls hustled to gather their meager possessions.

When the two men returned, Wookie is carrying a pistol grip pump — 16 gauge shotgun.

"Okay, you two wannabe crooked mutha' fucka's," roared Slick. "This is the deal I'm offering. We know about the diamonds, so give 'em up now or you'll not only be diggin' the grave for that dummy but you'll be diggin two more to go along with his. You know what I'm sayin' ?"

The women with bags in hand glared at the two men then glanced at each other.

"Give him the stash, Crystal," snorted Melody.

Crystal bugs her eyes, "I ain't given them creeps a mutha' fuckin' thing!"

Melody drops her bags and snatches one of Crystal's. It's an overnight case. She opens it and dumps out a five pound zip-lock bag filled with a rainbow of glistening stones. She kicks it over to Slick 's feet. He snatched the bundle and hoisted it up toward the ceiling light.

"Mutha' fuck!" howls Wookie.

"How about them apples?" decrees Slick. "Girls, it was nice doing business with ya, adios, hasta la vista...see ya!"

With that said the two men scurried over to the Cadillac and boned out.

"What the fuck, Melody! You just gave our fortune away!" Crystal shouts.

"I gave them fools a bag of synthetic rocks."

"Say-whaaat! You dirty bitch! You as scandalous as they come. You ain't told me jack until now, but I still love ya. So where's the real diamonds at?"

"They're hidden in the the trunk of your boyfriend's Road Runner, so just relax and let's get out of here before the police get here."

* * *

Wookie drove his CTS to an abandoned drive-in theater that was only used on weekends to hold community flea markets. The rear of the giant dilapidated screen was the backdrop to a hillside grave yard.

"What the fuck are you doin' Wookie?" squawked Slick as he takes a hit of his Humboldt county Cali skunk weed.

"I'mma give dude a proper burial, Slick."

"Proper my ass! Dump that fool in a ditch and let's beat it!"

"Call me superstitious if you like but it's bad karma if you kill a person and don't bury him. How would you like it if you died and your peeps just put you in a ditch? Besides, I know this graveyard. I use to play here when I was a kid. All we gotta' do is find a grave that's being prepped for a funeral. We dig a little deeper, dump and cover. Then the caretaker grave diggers will place a coffin right on top of the fool that's in my trunk."

Slick is high. He really doesn't care what Wookie does with the corpse, but he just likes to argue. "Boooyyy, you sharp. Now why didn't I think of that. Look-a-here, you crazy disrespectful mutha fucka, we betta not get busted up in this mutha fucken place. Cuz if we do, I swear you ass is grass, Wookie."

Wookie realized, by the way Slick was protesting, that he wasn't too fond about creeping around a graveyard in the dead of night. "Aight, aight, trust me, Slick. We're doing the right thing. We'll be in and out of that graveyard in record time."

It didn't take long for Wookie and Slick to find a freshly dug grave site that had been prepped for a funeral. There were a couple, but both of the locations were about a hundred feet from the office. Being that it was close to midnight, Wookie assured Slick that the night watchman was kicking back and probably watching some late night TV. But their problems were multiplied when they realized they didn't have a shovel.

"There's a toolshed at the rear of the office building," said Wookie, "right next to that stack of tombstones and plaques."

They took the long way around to avoid being seen by anyone who just might be peering from the building's front entrance. The toolshed location was a patio that was lit up by two street lamps, and within a matter of seconds, Wookie jimmied the lock and handed Slick a pair of shovels. Suddenly, they were startled by a voice coming from a squawk box.

"What are you doing out there?"

Instantly, the men spun around to see where the voice was coming from.

"Oh, boy, do you guys look silly! You know everything you're doing is being recorded on film! What-cha doin' with them shovels? You don't look like the type to be robbing from my graves!"

Both men were squinting their eyes in an attempt to see past the flood lights that were mounted on the roof.

"Our truck wheels are stuck in a ditch," said Wookie thinking fast. "We just needed to borrow these to dig our way out. We promise we'll bring'em right back."

"Oooh! Well hell, why don't I just call a tow truck to help you save some time."

"No-no! We got it under control," swears Slick.

"What! Are you guys on dope? Look fellas, you're lucky I'm just the fill-in night watchman, because if the regular was here, he'd have already called the cops. I ain't got nothing you want in here except a display of fresh coffins, so I suggest you put the shovels back and clear out, otherwise you may be seeing yourself on tomorrow's six o'clock evening news."

Benji Junior wasn't dead. He was just in a "Chakra", a transcendental state. Although the bullet grazed his skull, he was able to hold his breath for nearly seven minutes, which slowed his heart rate to a faint twenty beats per minute. It was a skill his parents taught him which he practiced to perfection since he was just a boy. He used his Third Eye, the imaginary point in the middle of his forehead. It allowed him to tap into his subconscious and float into a void somewhere in outer space.

His father also owned a Cadillac CTS, so it was easy for Benji to find the latch that opened the trunk from inside. Within a matter of seconds, he freed himself from captivity and vanished before his captors returned.

* * *

CHAPTER TWELVE

Crystal Melody

WE SLIPPED OUT of the Bahamas under the cover of darkness on a Friday night. We took a direct flight to Los Angeles and a Jet Blue to SFO, the Port of San Francisco. Miss Kenny's family leased us a furnished condo in a gated community. It was one of the real estate holdings his family owned. I decided to lay low until we got our shit together and our ducks in a row. Besides, my pit Mugsy, was alive and well and that's all I really needed to know. There's a lot of funny things that happens while you're in the game. The money comes easy but you can't sit on it or leave it in one place for very long. We got through customs with fifty stacks. Fifty thousand was just a portion of Bobbie Ray's carpetbag money, but we had to answer a lot of questions, so we gave them receipts that proved we'd done some gambling.

Hindsight is usually right. We should have taken Ray and Jimmy's advice, by flying to Europe or Ghana and enjoyed the fruits of our diamond heist. For now though, I'm just sun-bathing from a second floor terrace, thinking over all this shit. Wearing a spaghetti-string bikini, rubbing sunblock on my legs I notice two old-geezers gawking and checking me out.

"Cathy!"

"Yeah, what!"

She was snoozing on the living room couch and I think I woke her up. Cat sashayed her way over to me. She was wearing a green and white polka dot swim suit, showing off her sexy belly. The tropic sea air did her some good. She lost a few pounds.

"Say, Cat, you think Ray played us out of pocket with that story about his connects getting' swooped on?"

"What-the-heck! Why you just now bringing that up?"

"I'm just asking for your opinion, Obijwon, cuz you's my only hope."

Cat's about to fire up a cigarette, so she lights one for me as well, then blows a stream of smoke.

"Ha, give me some credit, Roxanne. I don't think so, but you know how the game go. It's a dog-eat-dog-world. Little fish get eaten by the big fish, and things seldom ever go as we plan them. You just gotta' go with the flow, Baby Girl," Cat said.

"True-That. And protect yourself at all times," I added.

"Righteous."

"Although I think we did a wise thing by transferring most of the cash into Swiss Bank accounts."

"Humph, yes yes, that was your play and a smart one too," Cat said.

We gave each other a high-five.

"Let's just hope none of them FBI hackers, trackers, nor baggers can figure us out."

"Oh, I ain't worried," replied Cat. "Them Bahamian banks are a good decoy. We'll just slow the way we roll and see what happens next."

The ringtone on Cat's cell phone played a chorus from a Caribbean hit... that Bob Marley xylophone shit. She liked it, but I didn't. It was Tommy Boy answering a message she'd left on his phone, so Cat turned up the volume so I could hear.

Tommy said he had an important message for the two of us but didn't want to discuss it over the phone. He wanted to set up a meeting place.

"No can do, Bubba," answered Cat. "You got to come up with somethin' betta than that, youngster. What's the skinny?"

"No, for reals, Miss. Wilson, square biz OG!"

Then someone abruptly takes control of his phone, "Cathy?"

"Yes."

"Cathy Wilson?"

"I just said yeah!! What's up?"

"This is My Lai. Is Roxanne nearby because I need to talk to her?"

"Me Lie!" Cat's blue eyes widen. They're the size of silver dollars. She hands me the phone.

"Blackwell, here. What's up trick! An' before you get ta snivelin', let me warn you...whatsoever you got to say in the next minute had betta be good, cuz if it ain't, Cunt, I'm hanging up on you!"

"Look, girlfriend, I had no choice. I had to move when I did because I was ordered to. Trust me, I wasn't trying to skate on ya'll."

"Ordered to? What kind of crock of shit are you sayin', Me Lie!"

"Hash Patel, the owner of the Thrift Store strip mall, hired me to set up the diamond heist."

"Hold-up!" I screeched. Cat looked over at me. She observed my shocked expression, but if looks could kill, My Lai would be dead "Bang!" right over the phone.

"Okay, we'll agree to meet with you, but on our terms, you dig?" I gave My Lai some bogus instructions so we had time to check her out and make sure she wasn't being tailed or setting us up. We'd only been in town for a week so Cat and I had to put some safe guards in place. I called Esquire Karrene and wired her a fifty thousand dollar retainer and sent Nasty Bill an additional twenty-five grand. It was a lot more than I owed him but if we go stuck in the slammer at least I could count on him to do a little runnin' for me. I didn't call Ray because I wasn't sure I could continue to trust him. He had ties with too many connects and when things start to fuck-up that's when people start tellin' on each other.

The mission was carried out in two separate rides. Cat had leased a silver Bentley Continental GT and I was sporting a black Ashton Martin. We had My Lai make her first pit stop at a Stanford Shopping Mall. I watched her arrive and leave as Cat phoned her to a new location. After a few more drills we all met up at a golf country club off Woodside Road in Redwood City. Hey, we could of kept this up all day, but if My Lai was hooked up with the FEDs, it wouldn't have made much difference 'cause eventually they'd figure it all out. So, Cat and I were doing our best just to stay one step ahead.

Being that it was late September, the Autumn leaves on most trees had begun to change, but the afternoon was still summer-like weather, a mild seventy degrees. We hooked up in the clubhouse patio, which was glass enclosed with a high arced ceiling. There were lots of spider plants dangling from the rafters. A cascade of ivory plants snaked around slim metallic poles, and potted wandering jews were stationed like some alien guards beside every table.

My Lai had gained some weight. It was the first time I'd seen her in Spartan heels and a backless yellow chiffon summer dress. Her hair was still slightly butch but she was letting it grow out. She looked hella cute though.

"How you doin'?" said Cat using her best improv of a Wendy Williams salute.

My Lai's face showed signs of strain. We each gave her a hug and let her know we wanted to give her the benefit of the doubt and still be her friend, but we needed to be convinced. We were anxious to hear her case.

"I be doin' a lot better if I find them mutha fuckin' bitches who ripped me off!" she huffed.

Cat and me sat facing her with blank stares, because we didn't know where My Lai was coming from. We ignored the comment momentarily. We ordered a few drinks and lit up some smokes.

"Me Lie," I said looking straight into her kite shaped brown eyes, "who ripped you off and what did they take?"

"Wait a minute," interrupted Cat, "you told us on the phone that Hash Patel, the owner of the Thrift Mall hired you, right?"

My Lai took a drag off her cigarette and answered, "Un hun, that's what I said." She was nodding her head and letting the cigarette smoke escape through her nostrils. "Yeah, the Patel man hired me but he didn't want to help with any of the details on how I should perform the heist. He wanted to stay clear of that in case he was required to do a lie detector test. The only thing he did to help me succeed was make sure that the right set of keys was within my grasp. However, I was so nervous the day we went in there, that I made three impressions."

"Okay," said Cat frowning and biting her bottom lip. I could tell she was searching for holes in My Lai's confession. "So, you got us to help you steal the man's own diamonds just so you could give them back? So, what was your cut and what was Bones' cut, 'cause based on what you're saying he must've been in on the deal from the start?"

My Lai's face faded a shade lighter. I could tell she was uncomfortable under Cat's scrutiny.

"Ease up," I said to Cat. "Let her tell it."

My Lai continued, "Bones, he not smart. I double cross him because of what he did to my father. The Patel family is connected to Las Vegas mafia. I don't know how deep but Bones owed Hash a lot of money so he had him taken out. I don't care 'cause it's Bones' fault. My job was to make sure Bones hired a good crew to see that the heist comes off without a hitch."

"A decoy," I blurted out.

"Yes, that," My Lai said.

"Well, if he had Bones killed then he killed Wilma too," I said.

"Yes, I'm deeply sorry for her, but I had no way of knowing they'd be together when it happened. Patel just thinks of it as collateral damage.

"Well-hell," piped Cat "why didn't you just do the heist all by yourself? Poor-ass Wilma, she just had to be in the wrong place at the wrong time."

"To be honest, I was a little scared of these people and I still am," My Lai said.

"Why is that?" I asked

My Lai blows another plume of smoke, crushes out her cigarette and sighs, "Because I was supposed to sit on the stones until Patel sent me word to bring them back. The half of million in cash was my payment as well as diamonds I split with you. His angle was to collect the insurance money and still keep the stones. Giving up a few million dollars in diamonds was only pocket money for him."

"Okay, I get your drift," I said, "so someone ripped off the stash of diamonds you were holding for Hash Patel."

"Yeah, a hooker."

"A hooker!" Cat and I both reply.

"That's right. I was hiding out in the town of Lebec, right outside of Bakersfield, when I took in this hooker I was trying to help out. Long story short, she and another chick and maybe a guy ripped me off while I was on an errand outside of town. But I got them all on film."

My Lai reached into her cheap imitation of a Gucci bag and pulls out the latest Samsung video cellphone. We scoot out chairs together and check out the screen.

"Stop, right-there!" I snapped.

"Okay."

"Go up...now come down...stop right there." I take a closer look. I don't recognize the girls but the guy I know, "That's Slick!"

"Slick? Who in the hell is, Slick?" clamored Cat.

"Slick is the guy that first got me started in the business. He taught me most of what I know today about hookin a monk. Me Lie, so the hooker you was taking care of was Slick's bitch?"

"Yeah, that's right him," says My Lai pointing.

"So where is them hoodlums at right now?" inquired Cat.

"I don't know for certain but I think they may be in the South Bay Area, because I got a license plate number to a Road Runner they were driving. I had it checked out and it belongs to an 'Anthony Moore'. He's an insurance investigator. He lives in Willow Glen, a suburb in San Jose."

* * *

Slick and Wookie didn't care nothing about Benji. They figured that if he's wiley enough to escape his burial, then surely an artful dodger knew better than to run his mouth to the police. Besides, they assumed he had to be a peeping somebody, because unless you're a crack addict or a neighborhood snitch, nobody hangs out in the middle of the night and get's cracked lurking beside someone's window. Their triumphant celebration was premature but they didn't know it yet, because their cache of diamonds had to be checked out by Wookie's boss, the pawnshop broker.

It was 9:00 p.m. and Larkin's Pawnshop had just closed when the two men banged on the glass of the oak stained door. An old man shuffled slowly towards the door.

"Mr. Larkin! It's me, Wookie," he declared with glee. "I got somethin' for you to check out. It won't take but a minute of your time".

Larkin opened the door with practiced caution. He gripped a pistol in his left hand. It was a Glock 17, a serious weapon. It was light and fit comfortably in the palm of even the smallest hand. But the old man had to be careful not to let his finger slip over the hair trigger, because he once reached for it too quickly and shot himself in the ass.."BANG!" It was a heart burst of an explosion, a nine-millimeter muzzle flash that he felt but didn't see.

"Damn you, Wookie," Larkin said in a gruff voice. "Why you come by so late and who's that with you?" He was looking at Slick over the top of his wire rimmed glasses. He takes notice of the greasy brown paper bag in Wookie's hand.

"He's cool, Boss. He's a local and a very good friend of mine."

After slamming three deadbolts behind them, the door was secured, then Larkin grabs the crumpled bag that's shoved into his hand. He shuffles over to the counter and the two men follow.

"What you got here...some rocks?" asked the old man with a sly wink and a grin.

Wookie returns the smile. His eyes are sparkling like emeralds. He got behind the counter with Larkin, reaches under the counter, and comes out with a square yard of fabric. It's an olive green felt material.

Larkin rips open the paper bag, "Oh-my!" his barely audible voice was more like a whimper than a statement of surprise. "Jeeze, will you look at that."

Slick and Wookie cackle. They're grinning from ear to ear.

Larkin's pale nimble fingers disappear into his vest pocket. He fishes out his jeweler's eyepiece, while Wookie uses a box-cutter and slits the plastic bag.

"Bring me the desk lamp, Wookie, cause I'll be needin' more light." Larkin spreads the stones over felt like a coffee bean farmer admiring a fresh harvest. There appears to be thousands of stones. The old man's Parkinson's disease hand trembles as he cuffs the diamonds while everyone watches them cascade through his fingers, a shimmering rainbow of colors, similar to a sunset gleaming off a rocky mountain waterfall. Larkin repeats the ritual several times, a bright broad smile is stretched across his haggard face. Some of the gem stones bounce from the counter to the floor.

"Get those, Slick!" barked Wookie.

"I got 'em."

"Okay, fellas," said Larkin choosing and examining several gems. Wookie and Slick stood perfectly still.

"Hmm..." the old man mumbles to himself. Then he sets the diamonds aside and goes through the ritual again, then again, at least several times, but he's not smiling any more. He clears his throat, sets the eyepiece on the counter, pulls a white handkerchief from his pocket, and wipes perspiration from his brow, "Synthetics."

"What'd you say, Boss?"

"I hate to rain on your parade, fellas, but these stones aren't real. They're imitations, good ones I might add."

"Imitations!" howls Slick. He reached over the counter and snatched Larkin by the lapels of his coat as dozens of diamonds tumbled to the floor.

"Wait, Slick! Don't hurt him!"

"He's lying to us, Wookie! Don't you see that!" Slick shouted, as his sparkled eyes turned murky red.

"No, no! I'm not lying," declares Larkin. "Why would I lie? Tell him, Wookie!" Both of the old man's hands were shaking and his cataract eyes displayed his fear.

Slick 's firm grip tightend on Larkin's coat, and he begin choking.

"Let'em go, Slick," pleaded Wookie. "He's telling us the truth, Brah'! I know him. He ain't lying, man. He wants to make money just like us."

Slick finally released Larkin from a strong hold. His enameled fingernails were hard as steel.

"Look fellas," said Larkin, keeping his eyes mostly on Slick as he attempted to straighten out his coat collar and two freshly torn lapels. "Yeah, they're worth a little something, but they're fakes made to look real. They're only good for costume jewelry, which is pretty much useless to me."

Both men realize the old man's words are earnest. Wookie is built like a Mandingo, a brave African Warrior, but at that moment, he looked as if he's about to cry.

"Look, fellas," said Larkin trying to spin a solemn situation into glee, "not all is lost. I'll give you five hundred for the whole lot."

Slick is still seething. After hearing what Larkin said his head bobbles until it hits his chest, then he pounds both fists into the counter and says, "THAT DIRTY BITCH!" He spins abruptly on his heels and walks away.

"Hey boss," consoles Wookie, "forget about it. You can have those, okay. Look, we gotta run. I'll check back with ya' in a couple days."

Wookie pats Slick on his left shoulder. "Come-on, Slick. Let's go smoke us a bat."

Pawn broker Larkin exhales a great sigh of relief as the two men leave. He shuffles behind them and triple-locks the door.

* * *

I like to take calculated risk, but I don't care for much drama. The underlying problem was — My Lai's life was hanging in the balance and perhaps mine's and Cathy's were as well. It was becoming apparent that if we didn't meet Hash Patel's deadline and return the bulk of diamonds by October 31st, we were certain his goons would hunt us down.

Eventually, we got our act together and devised a solid plan. Staking out a couple of Agent Moore's homes, we waited for Mr. Opportunity to present itself and catch two birds in the bush or one in each hand. We'd hoped them scuzzy-ass bitches had made their last mistake, because we weren't allowing them any means of escape.

* * *

"Where are we going in such a damn hurry, Crystal?"

"I got to get Pookie his car back. That man's gonna' have a hissy fit if I don't get it back to him today. He act worse than a be-aatch. I done kept the damn thing for almost a month."

"Pookie, huh?", Melody said with a grin.

"Yeah, I got tah' butter him up just a little bit for being so nice. That way I can get him to loan me another car. You know what I'm sayin'? He got five of 'em."

"You wicked, Crystal."

"Oh, you playa' hatin' on me?" Crystal flips the auto's blinker and makes a left turn.

"No, I ain't hatin', but I wonder what Slick and Wookie are gonna do when they figure out those diamonds are fakes?"

"Ha! Them ninja's gon' blow a piston, a gasket, and a muffler," said Crystal giggling mostly to herself. "Gimme' some dap, White Bread, cuz we some bad mamma jammas!" The hookers bumped fists. Crystal's clowning around helped Melody to stop worrying so much.

She cranked up the stereo's volume. "Sharlene" an oldies Gap Band C.D.'s blew thru' the speakers

At 11:00 p.m. they pulled up in the driveway of a vintage 60's track home, which was an above-average-income neighborhood. Ever since the microprocessor computer chip boom hit in Silicon Valley, the cost of living had soared. Most of the 'Leave it to Beaver' neighborhoods were no longer prime living spaces unless you worked for a technology company, because the price of renting or buying a home in the area had climbed exorbitantly.

The property was one of three that Agent Moore owned. He had a home on the Eastside near the Bayshore's 101 Freeway, and two and a half acres outside the town of Morgan Hill. It was inhabited by three Black Angus bulls grazing mostly on the next-door neighbor's yard. When you stare through a window long enough, you see things you shouldn't see. My Lai and Cat were staking out the Willow Glen Home, and I was posted-up near the one in the East. We used our cell phones to text and instant message each other.

◆◆◆

CAT, WHAT THEY DOIN?

◆◆◆

THEY JUST SITTIN AND TALKIN

◆◆◆

"I don't know, Crystal. How do you expect me to trust somebody you've only met a month ago?"

"Chill-out, Mel. I'm good at readin' people. It comes with the turf, so let's take him the jewel sack so we can make us some 'real' money."

◆◆◆

ROXANNE THEY RINGIN THE DOOR BELL. NOW THE DOOR IS OPEN AND THEY JUST WALKED INSIDE.

♦♦♦

WHO LET EM IN?

♦♦♦

A BLACK DUDE.
I CANT SEE HIS FACE.
WHAT'S GOIN' DOWN ON YOUR END?

♦♦♦

I DONT KNOW.
BUT I THINK I'M IN THE MIDDLE OF A BLOCK PARTY
AND I THINK THIS IS A GANG NEIGHBORHOOD

♦♦♦

WHY YOU SAY THAT?

♦♦♦

CUZ MOST EVERYBODY WEARIN RED!

♦♦♦

HELL, THEY COULD BE 49ER FANS.

♦♦♦

THAT MAY BE TRUE,
BUT I THINK THEY'RE BLOODS.

♦♦♦

WHAT 'CHA WEARIN?

♦♦♦

BLACK ON BLACK OVER BLACK.

♦♦♦

YOU COOL THEN, BUT BE CAREFUL

♦♦♦

THOUGHT I WASN'T.

♦♦♦

"Girls, let me take your jackets," offered Agent Moore. The girls were wearing their grunge wear, windbreakers, sweatshirts, jeans and tennis shoes. Moore continued, "Get comfortable ladies, this won't take but a second. The bar is right over there. Fix yourselves a drink," he urged. Moore was wearing a grey frayed suit and a white shirt with no tie. His boots were gray lizard skins. He wore lifts so he could look taller. Then he disappeared through the kitchen and returned with an oversized hat box. He walked over to the fireplace and opened the flue. Lodged inside was a hefty green plastic bindle wrapped with strips of grey neoprene tape. He yanked it free and carried it over to the bar.

The girls were downing shots of Makers 46, a high proof Kentucky bourbon. They watched Moore slice open the bag and fill the box with stacks of mostly twenty dollar bills. He was whistling along with "The

William Tell Overature", a once popular symphonic tune that he was playing on his stereo.

"How much is that?" asked Melody.

"Oh, about...a hundred thousand, plus or minus a buck or two," Agent Moore said

"That's not enough."

Agent Moore stops his meticulous process and shoots Melody a blank stare.

"What'cha talkin' 'bout, Mel!," says Crystal. "Honey, this ain't no time for a debate. The man is offerin' us cash money for these rocks, an- -".

Melody yanks Crystal by the arm and spins her around. It's the only way she can get Crystal to shut up. Then she whispers something Agent Moore can't hear. His thin black eyebrows are arched way past normal. He cuts off the symphony music and replaces it with an old school Jamaican tape, "The Rubicons". The lead singer's alto soprano voice along with the back-up singers lullaby is a surreal fantasy to the listener.

Crystal turns to look back at him.

"Give us a second, Pookie. We'll be right back," she said yielding a wry grin.

[Music] ALL OF MY LIFE I'VE DREAMED OF YOU......(dreamed of you)

YOU'RE LIKE A DREAM...THAT'S COMING TRUE....(coming true)

They take a few steps and stop in front of the fireplace.

"Look, Crystal, the pawn broker gave me ten grand for twelve stones and those were just the blue ones. I've read that the browns and reds go for a lot more. Your guy is trying to get over on us."

"Are you serious," cried Crystal.

"Hell-yes, I'm serious. There's hella diamonds in our sack."

[Music] SO MANY TIMES I'VE THOUGHT THAT YOU WERE MINE...WHY CAN'T I MAKE YOU SEE THAT YOU ARE EVERY PART OF ME...AND I

LOVE YOU...

(can't you tell I'm in love with you)
WHY WOULD I LEAVE YOU?
(can't you see that I love you)
"I don't know, Mel?"

"Come-on, girl, it's not gonna' hurt to at least make a reasonable counter offer."

"Girls, is everything all right?" probed Moore as he gingerly walks toward them with a fresh shot-glass of bourbon in each hand.

The girls take the drinks and Crystal downs the fiery spirit and pats her chest bone with her left hand, "Oooou, that's some good cognac, Pookie." Crystal is tipsy and Agent Moore is doing his best to get the hookers drunk.

[Music] IF I LOVE YOU...
(I'm really in love with you)
WHY WOULD I LEAVE YOU?...
(don't you see that I love you)

Agent Moore reverts his attention to Melody. She's examining the booze as though it's got ricin in it, a vegetable poison that comes from the castor oil plant. Like arsenic, it's a masquerade poison.

Finally, Melody finds her courage, "We want five hundred 'K' and not a penny less. And we want it tonight," she adds without raising her eyes to look at him.

[Music] IF I LOVE YOU...
(I'm really in love with you)
WHY WOULD I LEAVE YOU?...
(I'm really in love with you)

Agent Moore smiles and Crystal wobbles over to a barstool, lights a cigarette, then sits down. Other than the music, there's dead silence between them for what seems like a hundred minutes.

"Okay," said Agent Moore in a condescending tone, "we can do that, but first let me make a call."

Melody watches him with weary eyes as he walks through the doorway that leads to the kitchen.

♦♦♦

HEY CAT, ITS ME....WHATS GOING ON?

♦♦♦

THEY STILL INSIDE.

♦♦♦

YOU ALL RIGHT?

♦♦♦

YEAH I'M SAFE, BUT I DONT THINK THEY BE
COMING HERE, SO I'M 0N MY WAY.

♦♦♦

OKAY, SEE YA.

♦♦♦

'TAP-Tap-Tap!' A fist wearing a class ring flashed across the car's passenger side window. Two females wearing hoodies, one burgundy and the other a bright red were trying to see inside my car. I hit the window's power button and let it down far enough for a two-inch gap.

"Who are you, lady, and what you doin' in the shadows like this?"

"Yeah, is you the Popo?" said the other girl.

I could smell the stench of liquor and chronic on their breaths. I pushed the Ashton Martin's ignition switch and the engine instantly purred, "I was just leaving," I said.

Then, the girl closest to the window said, "Oh-yeah!" and from under her sweats she whipped out a snub-nose .38 caliber pistol. I popped the clutch and my tires screeched as I fishtailed outta' there in a flash. TWO shots rang out... One at me, and the other in the air.

◆◆◆

[Music] MAYBE I FAILED TO MAKE YOU UNDERSTAND....(understand) HOW MUCH YOU MEAN TO ME, YOU'RE PART OF EVERY PLAN...(every plan)

"Give me some dap, girlfriend," said Crystal slurring her words, "Cuz you is a baaad mamma jamma"

Melody doesn't smile because she's worried. Her gut tells her she really shouldn't trust this dude. "I don't know Crystal. Maybe I've gone too far?"

"Naw-naw, we cool, girlfriend, and Pookie knows it. You just wait an' see. He'll fix everything. We'll be rolling in dollars tonight, tah-he-he."

(Music) IN EVERY WAY YOU GET ME THROUGH EACH AND EVERY DAY...BUT STILL IT'S HARD FOR ME, SOME DAY YOU'LL KNOW...

When Agent Moore walks back in the living room, he's wearing a brown derby, a black London Fog trench, and brown driving gloves. He's slowly buttoning the collar on the coat, then tugging at his gloves, "Let's roll girls."

"Where are we going?" asked Melody.

"Not far, just up the road," said Moore, as he opens the front door. Crystal practically runs past Moore, but Melody hesitates.

[Music] CAUSE I LOVE YOU...

(I'm really in love with you)

WHY WOULD I LEAVE YOU?...

Agent Moore glares at Melody, "You want your money don't cha'?" his brown ferret like eyes flit from Melody to Crystal, than back to Melody again.

"Come-on, Mel, let's roll!" cried Crystal stomping her feet.

Moore hands them their jackets. Crystal has got the box of money tucked under her arm and Melody clings to the satchel of diamonds

[Music] IF I LOVE YOU

(I'm really in love with you)

WHY WOULD I LEAVE YOU?...

They abandon the Road Runner and squeeze into Agent Moore's Jag'.

The ride was short, about two miles. They cruised quietly down a wide graveled street with nothing but mansions, tall oaks, and sycamores on either side. The street was littered with freshly fallen autumn leaves.

They parked and climbed out. The moonless sky was indigo blue. The air was cool and crisp. They passed through a brick archway and climbed twenty cobblestoned steps. Finally, they reached an ornate set of copper plated doors. Agent Moore pushed the doorbell and a door-slot opened only large enough to see the bridge of a nose and a pair of narrow brown eyes. A tall burly man wearing a shark skin suit stepped out. He was leering at everyone like he was Robert De Niro or some kind of gangster guy.

"If you're carrying heat, you gotta' leave it with me," he echoed in a resonant baritone. Moore quickly reached inside his coat and handed him a .357 magnum pistol. The girls followed protocol and gave up their weapons as well.

"Follow that path," the goon said pointing. "There's a hutch in the back."

The hutch was an adobe building with a flat brick tiled roof. They stepped onto a dimly lit porch, where the screened door was open. They all walked inside.

♦♦♦

CAT...WHERE ARE YOU?

♦♦♦

THEY MOVED SO WE MOVED.
WE OVER IN THE BURBANK HOOD,
YOU KNOW THE OLD SCHOOL MANSIONS.

♦♦♦

WHAT STREET?

♦♦♦

HANCHET.

♦♦♦

OKAY, I'M ALMOST THERE.

♦♦♦

There were three men waiting inside the building's single room. They were big men with grim faces. In the floor's middle was a makeshift table supported by two wooden saw horses which took up a lot of space. The floor was covered with brown plastic tarp and as Crystal and Melody took timid steps, the tarp kept sticking to the soles of their shoes. The semi-darkness of the room cast only shadows. Someone shut the door and slid a two-by-four in place. A dimmer switch was rotated and the room was flooded with a blinding light which caused the girls to squint.

There was an assortment of shiny cutting tools on the table and others on hooks along the walls.

By the time Crystal and Melody realized that Agent Moore was nowhere in sight, the panic had reached their eyes and the music they heard back at Moore's home was still in their heads...

...CAUSE I LOVE YOU!

...(I'm really in love with you!}
...WHY WOULD I LEAVE YOU?
...(I'm really in love with you!) ...IF I LOVE YOU,
...(I'm really in love with you!)
...WHY WOULD I HURT YOU?!!!

But it was too late. Both girls were trembling. There was no time to go berserk. The hutch was soundproofed. It didn't matter...no one was going to hear their muffled screams. A stark shockness had overcome them...they could gurgle but not scream..

[MUSIC] IF I LOVE YOU!!!
CAUSE I'M REALLY IN LOVE WITH YOU!!!
WHY WOULD I HURT YOU?!!!

♦♦♦

I spotted Cat and My Lai's ride, and I passed them and parked a half-block ahead. I watched from my rearview camera.

♦♦♦

WHERE ARE THEY?

♦♦♦

IN THE BROWN BRICK MANSION.
THE ONE YOU PASSED ON YOUR LEFT.

♦♦♦

IT'S TOO DARK...I DIDNT NOTICE.

♦♦♦

HEY, HOLD UP...SOMEONES COMING...

ROXXY

IT'S AGENT MOORE!!!
YOU BETTA' DUCK CUZ HE'S COMING
YOU'RE WAY!!!

* * *

CHAPTER THIRTEEN

Mugsy

I CAME INTO THIS 'Monster Heist' thinking it would be simple, yet that queasy feeling in my stomach wouldn't go away. Bones and Wilma are dead and maybe Crystal and Melody too. We waited until dawn and them bitches never showed. Around 5:00 a.m. a black SUV with three men deep rolled out the brick mansion's gated driveway. We still don't know if that was Hash Patel's main house or just one of many, and we didn't know what he looked like, because whenever My Lai heard from him it was only by text or voice-mail. The fact that he was the owner of the Thrift Drug Mall and the family head, it was unlikely we'd catch him just hanging out at a local sports bar.

"A diamond for your thoughts?" I said to My Lai. The three of us were hanging out, having drinks and airing out my Terra Cotta Heights apartment. At least Mugsy was happy and my neighbors, who'd been watching over him for the last several months, were also very pleased. But, My Lai never got a chance to answer my teaser because the FED's came knocking. We quickly hid her in my bedroom closet while Cat and I were escorted downtown. They said we weren't under arrest. They wanted to ask us a few questions and it wouldn't take long. As usual, THEY LIED!

Months before the Thrift Drug Mall diamond heist had come into play, the Patel's were being closely watched by the FED's from their Nevada division. Apparently, Hash Patel had some serious business ties with the Mora Family, who had a lot of money invested in Reno's and Las Vegas' casinos, motels and brothels. The Family was originally from Buffalo, New York, and back in the 50's they were aligned with well known crime families in Chicago and Philadelphia. After their migration to the West Coast, they established a franchise 'Finance and Loan' company in the South Bay Area, predominately San Jose. They invested several million dollars into Hash Patel and his enterprises as well.

During the mid-seventies, at the height of Silicon Valley's electronic boom, Hash Patel was a top flight microprocessor engineer from New Delhi, the capital of India. Hash ran a startup company, a semiconductor brokerage, which warehoused mass amounts of silicon chips and electronic components. His prices undercut other vendors by sometimes as much as sixty percent. He used a bartering system with some of the larger companies like Intel, Fairchild, and National Semiconductor. Ambitiously trading those commodities for synthetic gems and inferior diamonds used for cutting, drilling, or grinding tools. Hash rapidly accumulated stockpiles of topaz from Brazil, rubies from Thailand, and emeralds from Columbia.

Hash was not a selfish man. Besides keeping a very diverse financial portfolio, and maintaining his loyalty to the Mora's, he made sure his family members benefited from his shrewd business mind. He had the Thrift Drug Mall built especially for them.

After listening to the FED's mountain of information, which made no sense, Cat and I realized the agents were only fishing for more information on the Patels because they really had no case. At the time of our interview, they hadn't known that Hash held the rank of captain in the Mora Organization, which gave him the authority to order hits or personally take people out. And just when we thought the interview was over, in walks two more agents. One of them handed me, then Cat, a business card. They were private dicks, Rob Cash and Ashley Jensen from Sunset Investigations. The Cash guy was a handsome — six foot, copper toned, with gold trim on two of his front teeth. He had a neatly trimmed chin-strap goatee. Ashley Jensen had hypnotic blue eyes and natural shoulder length blond hair. She was a petite five-foot-two. When I read the name, Cash, I asked for a time-out and used Cat's cell phone. It took a few calls to track down Karrene.

"What's up Blackwell?"

"You tell me!" I yammered.

Karrene sighs, "Get to the point. Court is about to reconvene. I haven't got much time."

"You got any P.I.'s in your family?"

"Yes, my brother owns Sunset Investigations. Why?"

"Never mind...'CLICK'!"

Cash and his girl-pal were laid back with their questioning early on, but later their questions got more intense. They had film on Cat and I, which was taken from the drug store security cameras. Based on what they shared, there was nothing incriminating about the film's footage, except for the ruckus Wilma and Cat caused that 'Monday' morning on aisle number one, a little past ten o'clock. According to the footage, I was seen near My Lai right before she slipped into the back room and came out wearing a Thrift Drug Store smock.

"Do either of you know this woman?" asked Jensen pointing to My Lai's image.

"No," we answered, both shaking our heads from left to right.

"Why do you ask?" I challenged.

"There was a theft of highly valued personal property and we'd like to talk to this woman," replied Karrene's brother.

"Because?" mewed Cathy.

"Because we believe she's the guilty party in this crime," retorted Miss. Jensen.

"Oh"

"Oh, is all you can tell us?" parroted Jensen.

"As we stated earlier, we've never met her and we don't know who she is," I said.

"What about Benji Patel," countered Jensen.

"Who's that?" I asked

"The pharmacist," inserts Karrene's brother. "The film footage shows you were having what appeared to be an in-depth conversation at the same time the Asian woman walks up the staircase behind the counter and slips inside the main office."

"Hmm..." I pretend to think on it as though it happened too long ago to recall, "Oh, now I remember. He was trying to help me find some...oh, what was it..."

"Antihistamines."

"Yes, that's right. My sinuses clog sometimes, allergies, I guess."

"I see," said Jensen, as though she's competing for the lead role in a TV crime show. "So what were you doing in the pharmacist's storage closet on Wednesday, only a couple days later?"

"Beg your pardon?"

"The room next to the beverage cooler," answers Karrene's brother.

I smile, because he's checking my body language out while his girl-pal is trying to trip me up. Even though they claimed they had an image of a female entering the storage room, they weren't certain it was actually me because I wore a disguise. So I frown and shake my head as though I haven't a clue as to who they're talking about.

"Let me refresh your memory, Miss. Blackwell," persisted Jensen. This chick just wouldn't quit. She reached inside her shoulder bag and pulled out an iPad displaying the surveillance film.

"On Wednesday morning it was raining. You entered the store wearing a clear plastic raincoat. You unlocked the storage room, entered, then closed the door. Five minutes later the pharmacist followed you in. Then suddenly, you came bursting out the door and we believe that before going out you dialed 911."

"911?"

"Yes!" shouted Jensen.

Then Karren's brother takes over. "We have no film to show what's happened to the pharmacist inside, but when the paramedics arrived, they said he had a mild stroke and found him in a compromising position."

"What's that supposed to mean?" protested Cathy, trying to take some of the heat off me and give me a little time to think.

"It means his trousers were pulled down to his ankles," Jensen said sarcastically.

Cat and I both laugh simultaneously, then I pretend to realize it's inappropriate, so I clear my throat, "Sorry for him, and I hate to disappoint, but you've got the wrong gal."

Jensen wanted to press a little harder, but I wasn't about to allow these amateurs to do me in. Even if they assumed that me and the pharmacist had a fling or meeting of some kind. There was no real evidence to pin me or Cat to the diamond heist unless they could prove we knew My Lai. Besides, her identity was still a mystery to them, so oh well.

* * *

When we got back to my penthouse, the three of us realized our predicament was a little more serious than we first thought. My Lai made us a quart of Mai' Tai. Then we kicked back and made some critical plans.

"Did Agent Moore show his face at the inquisition?" asked My Lai.

"Hell-nah!" yelled Cat "That fool is working for Hash Patel. He ain't gonna' risk letting them two junior foot soldiers, who interviewed us, figure out where his loyalties lie."

"I think the P.I.'s were hired by someone else in the Patel family," I added.

"Why?" said My Lai.

"I don't know. Maybe there's some distrust within the ranks."

"Right now, that's the least of our concerns, cuz it ain't gonna' help us even if there was a feud goin' on. What we gotta' do is figure out what our next move should be!" bellowed Cat.

"That's obvious," replied My Lai, "we know Hash has got his diamonds back but he doesn't know we know, so he's going to stick by his deadline. Besides, we all aided in the heist, so he can't afford to let any of us off the hook."

"That means he's gonna' have us killed," murmured Cat while sucking on the ice cube in her drink.

"He's gonna try!" I fired back.

"That's why we can't afford to sit around and wait. Hash and none of his goons know about my hideaway in the desert. We can chill out there because I got everything in place that we will need to survive."

"Can I bring Mugsy?"

"Of course, you bring whatever you like."

*   *   *

We're traveling light. Besides Mugsy, I take an overnight bag and only a few essentials. I abandon everything else, because wherever we go I can always buy more stuff.

Before beginning our trek though, I couldn't resist, my pussy was yearning for Ray, so I called Karrene to try and make contact with him. She told me Ray was vacationing with his wife and she doesn't know if they're in the Bahamas or someplace else. She encouraged me to check back with her in a few days. I thanked her and proceeded with my next move.

We were taking all the necessary precautions. My Lai bought a secondhand Ford truck with a mini-camper shell. She advised Cat to leave the Caddy but Cat refused to leave her classic 1955 ragtop behind. "It's a collector's item and it's her baby", she said. She practically throws a conniption fit, so we reluctantly let her have her way. We decided to travel the El Camino Real' because the storage room is along that route.

I was once told the El Camino Real' (The Royal Roadway) was built by the Spanish missionaries during the 17th century. The road connects the Spanish missions which were built in every town from San Diego to San Francisco. There were supposed to be close to two dozen missions built along California's coastline. Before freeways came into existence, the Old El Camino Real' was the most traveled road in the state's history.

Our journey took us north before we headed south. We made a pit stop in the city of San Mateo to pick up Cathy Wilson's car. Her mechanic had it stored in a shipping container right outside of Half Moon Bay. We drove up to the attendant's booth, and Cat paid the balance on the rental fee. Opening the barrier, the attendant let her inside the fence. We watched her walk towards the brown and white rust covered container and remove a lock. We heard the iron and steel creak as she slid open the bay door. A gray sailor's tarp covered the Caddy. She removed it, opened the driver's side door and disappeared inside. The attendant left his both and opened the gate wide enough so the Caddy had plenty of room for an exit.

Suddenly, smoke and fire lept from the Caddy's tailpipe...and the ground rumbled before we heard the blast...

"KaaAHH-BOOOOOM!"

Our eardrums were instantly plugged, and it felt like they had burst. The attendant's body hurled, then smacked the side of our truck. There was fire and a black cloud of billowy smoke. Falling debris shattered our truck's windshield. Cathy's Caddy and two other containers were blown to smithereens.

My Lai and I bolted from our seats. I charged the leaping flames... I think I had lost it for a second... I was screaming Cathy Wilson's name at the top of my lungs. At that instant, I must have believed I could bring her back from death. My Lai tackled me from behind... I don't remember what happened next, but she must've slugged me... Because I was out cold. Then My Lai must have dragged me by my feet, because when I woke up my legs and arms were gravel scarred and the left side of my jaw was swollen.

I pulled down the Ford truck's visor and looked in the mirror. Black mascara was streaked across my face and my fiery red hair looked like it hadn't been combed in weeks.

"Where are we?" I groveled. I was feeling empty like I'd lost a lot of blood.

"We just passed through Maricopa. We've got another twenty-five miles before we reach Lebec.

I yawned and stretched my arms like the letter "Y".

"Damn, I feel like I've been asleep for six years," I said, still groggy.

"I gave you a pill," My Lai said.

"A sleeping Pill?"

"Yeah."

"Yuk," I smack my lips and try to swallow. My mouth has a nasty taste to it, and feels like I've been eating chalk.

"What about Cat?"

"I'm sorry, Roxanne, but there was nothing we could do. We had to get out of there before the police arrived."

"You got a cigarette?"

"Look in the glove box."

While I was searching, she handed me a silver flask. "Here, have a nip. You'll feel better."

"I took a swig. There was no burn. It went down real smooth, and it was fruity. I think it was Peppermint Schnapps. I reclined my head and within minutes fell back to sleep.

* * *

I'm dreaming...The water is warm, aqua green and translucent. I can see coral reefs and colorful tropical fish on the bottom... Then, I got tangled in some algae. It was brown instead of green. I see a body penned under a rock and stuck between a crevice. It was black and decomposed. The long brown hair was flowing. The skin had slipped.

Now, I could see the face. It was Cat. Her Oprah eyes were open. Her lips were pea green and extremely large... The corpse grabbed me by my ankles. I'm trying to swim but I can't. The corpse is pulling me deeper into the water. I'm swallowing water and I'm gasping for air... I felt a jolt. My heart was racing like I've never felt before. Startled, I awoke...

*   *   *

The Ford truck was not moving anymore, it felt like we were parked. "Where are we?" I murmured while looking over at My Lai.

You've been having dreams," she answered, her kite eyes looming, "but you're safe now. Look around you. This will be our home for a while."

I saw trees... shade trees, fruit trees, and a roof that looked like it was collapsed. It's got a door with holes in it and a pathway leading up to it. There was some kind of house but there were no windows and most of it was buried underground. I looked in the other direction, and I saw a well, two concrete wash basins, and a clothes line.

"You call this home?" I said, yawning and frowning all at the same time.

"Go on, get out. Stretch your legs and get some sun."

My Lai grabbed most of our stuff and disappeared somewhere inside.

*   *   *

I didn't know how many days had passed. My Lai stayed busy and I stayed in bed. It wasn't like me, but I had no drive or energy. Maybe, it was the heat, high 80's at least. My Lai was in the garden mostly. She said she was nursing a patch of purple-haired chronic. One day she brought me a blunt, and the smoke was good too. It lifted me right out of my funk. My aching heart felt a whole lot better so I went outside to join her in the garden. The dry-ass heat was mild that day, so we decided on a picnic.

My Lai's oasis had a little of everything: cherry red tomatoes, Japanese cucumbers, green snap-beans, baby red potatoes, garlic, green onions, yellow jalapenos, mustard greens, musk melons, and black berries. She even had a miniature pond with gold and white koi fish. The trees were gorgeous and they yielded lemons, oranges, almonds, and hazelnuts.

I began to see another side of My Lai, other than her cagey wit and shrewdness. Her work ethic impressed the hell out of me. She was reliable and very kind. I thought to myself, 'This Asian Chick is the real deal.' We had a fruit salad and I toasted some garlic bread over an outdoor grill. We got settled under the almond tree. Thank God there were no gnats flying around.

"You know we'll have to leave this country, Roxanne?"

"Yeah, I'm hip to it, but we're left without a choice, right?" My Lai's mind must have went somewhere else because she didn't respond. She was staring at a sand dune about a quarter mile out. "Where will you go, back to Vietnam"? "

"No, I've been away too long and I'm spoiled. I plan to live in Hong Kong until it is safe and I can do better,"

"What do you mean, safe?"

"From this day forward our lives will never be safe. Even in Hong Kong, I have to watch out for them who wear the dragon tattoo."

"Dragon Tattoo?" I say curiously.

"It's a club, a clique of hired contract killers."

"You mean mercenaries."

"Yeah, kind of like that."

"Well, maybe you should come with me to Switzerland."

"It doesn't matter where we go, sooner or later they find us."

"Humph, you just put a lot of drama on my mind and I hate drama."

"Well, forget about it."

We were silent with each other for what seemed like an hour. The sky was faded blue, and a few crows made chatter. Then My Lai offered me a fresh slice of melon. My first thought was she was trying to hit on me, but I'm not into chicks, so my thoughts went to Ray. I need to give Karrene another hollar. Then My Lai broke the silence.

"So, Switzerland is where your money is kept?"

"Yeah, most of it. I've plenty enough for the both of us, My Lai."

"You'd do that for me?"

"Of course, I haven't forgotten that those two hookers ripped you off."

"Okay, that's true. But first, let me show you something."

We walked over to a concrete basin.

"Here, help me push this," instructs My Lai. "Put your back against it and use your legs."

I followed her lead and we moved the tub three or four feet. The soil was damp underneath. Worms and black beetles got busy as they were trying to escape the sunlight. My Lai walked over to the lemon tree and picked up a shovel. She dragged the shovel's metal face over the topsoil at least three times. Before long, I saw the pattern of a rectangular box about three feet long by two feet wide. Again, she used the shovel to pry open the lid. Stuffed inside was a bulging brown potato sack. I helped her pull it out and it was kinda' heavy, maybe thirty pounds, so we carried it to the house.

Once inside, My Lai spread out a white sheet on the floor and used an army tactical knife to rip open the burlap bag. Then she dumped the contents out.

My mouth flew open like a Muppet's. I was looking at My Lai like I had something lodged in my throat.

My Lai lit a cigarette, took a puff and let it dangle from the left corner of her mouth, then she grinned.

Finally, I regained my voice. "Tell me those aren't Hash Patel's diamonds, ME LIE!"

She cracks the knuckles on her left hand, then laughed. But I wasn't feeling that anything was funny. I didn't know whether to hug this chick or choke her ass out. She saw that my complexion had paled but it didn't faze her.

"Now you understand why you or I can't remain here. And if we don't split up, we will surly die."

She offered me a Salem and we both sat down on the floor. Contemplating in silence, staring at the bags of diamonds, we filled the single room with smoke.

"Hash Patel's people did not take out Bones," explained My Lai. "Bones, he worked for more than one mob. He spreads his hustle to the highest bidder. Remember, he's the guy that knew how to make a cargo plane disappear on paper. Roxanne, the man had skills. There are different kinds of mafia organizations besides Italian. There's Russian mob, Irish mob, Jewish mob, Asian mob, Black mob and Latin/Mexican mob, just to name a few. Even my father, in his line of business, worked for the mob."

"So which mob did it?"

"Did what?"

"Take out Bones?"

"Oh, I think Jewish mob. When he cooked the books of the department store chain, the amount of time he did in prison was like a slap on the wrist, which pissed the owners off. The FED's stepped in and turned the company upside down. The company was doing illegal stuff and was hoping Bones and my father would take the attention away from them, but the FED's figured it out. The company lost their clout in the industry. They had to liquidate everything and start over in a different county and under a different name. You see, the state government only allows so many companies to compete in a certain locale. It's a circle of recycled money that constantly changes hands. If you're the new company on the block and you fuck up, the same companies who let you in will force you out," My Lai explained.

"So, the company that got forced out, had Bones taken out to send a message to anyone who might try to play them in the future?" I said.

"Something like that. Word travels fast and the mob can't lose face with other mobs, because it's bad for business all the way around. It makes them look weak, so sooner or later Bones had to go. I just helped him go a little sooner than he expected."

"You mean by taking the diamonds?" I ask.

"Yeah, something like that."

My Lai took the last puff on her cigarette, as mine was just sitting there smoldering in my hand, so I crushed it out. We both stared at the pile of dazzling stones.

"Okay, My Lai, I got one more question. How do you explain the two sets of diamonds?"

"Oh-that!" My Lai laughed, then grinned. "The synthetic gems were not mixed in with the real stones. They were marked separately. When I stayed overnight in the fabric store, I rearranged all the bags and hid a few of the real diamonds inside the Thrift Drug Store, as you already know, just in case something went wrong. Doing that was not part of the deal I made with Hash. I was hired to take all the diamonds out and sit on them until further instructions. I could not afford to lose them, so I planned for the worst possible scenario just in case."

"But you later told us you were paid in cash?"

"That's true, there was a stash of cash with the diamonds, and Melody took most of that, but while she was plotting against me, I sold a few thousand diamonds to a dealer in Santa Clarita and had the money wired to my Uncle's bank in Hong Kong."

"Oh, does he own a bank?"

"Not really, but something like that."

"What do you plan to do with these stones?" I ask.

"They're all yours if you want them. I can't take them. They're more trouble than they are worth," My Lai said.

"Why?"

"Because wherever you go they leave a trail, a bloody trail."

We stood and stretched. Then we both fell silent again. I looked around the room like I was still trying to decide. My Lai watched me with her arms folded as though she could read my mind.

"They're coming after us, you know," My Lai said in a serious tone.

"Yeah, I know. But please stop reminding me."

"We haven't got much time. I suggest you take the diamonds down to Bakersfield. There's a pawnbroker on Main Street. He'll give you a good price and enough cash to travel on. You can use my truck."

"Okay... When should I do that, first thing in the morning?"

"No! Go now, this afternoon. Get a room at the Holiday Inn. I'll meet you there tonight."

"How can you possibly do that without your truck?"

My Lai strutted over to the corner of the room, knelt down and began to loosen cinderblocks along the wall. I walked over to get a closer look. There was a passageway that placed us under a shed at the rear of the house. I followed her lead and we both had to manuver around a tarp covered vehicle before we reached the hinged single doorway that put us outside.

My Lai removed the tarp.

"Hey, that's nice... Real nice," I said, amazed and impressed with her. It was a 1969 Camaro, four speed, all white body with blue pin stripes bordering the hood and roof. The leather interior was dyed cobalt blue with a 396 engine block under the hood.

By 3:00 p.m. Mugsy and I reached Interstate 5, crossing the outer city limits of Bakersfield. Mugsy was happy. His little nub for a tail was trying to wag from side-to-side. I drove to a nice neighborhood where the homes appeared to have been owned by families with above average incomes. There were kids riding bikes and playing kick ball in a cul-de-sac. I made a U-turn, parked and let Mugsy out so he could handle his business and roam a little bit. He saluted a tree, then waddled over to where three little girls were having a tea party on a front yard lawn. I watched from my windshield with a tightness in my gut. While two girls were petting him, I waved a silent goodbye. Started the truck's engine and quietly crept away.

I was just about to turn a corner, when I glanced at the truck's side mirror and saw Mugsy running down the middle of the street. His little ears were pinned back. He was desperately trying to catch up to me. My heart caved inside my chest, and tears burst from my eyes. I wanted to stop, but it would be too dangerous to try and take him with me. I increased my speed, and began sobbing silently. Kids on bikes chased after him... Instantly, I knew he'd be loved and he'd be safe, but my sadness did not subside.

Leaving Mugsy was one of the hardest things I've ever had to do in my life. Even driving the truck became extremely difficult because I was truly heartbroken and my eyes were burning from the tears. My vision became blurred and it felt like I was driving in a thick cloud of fog. Mugsy was all I had, and now I no longer had him. What was I to do?

CHAPTER FOURTEEN

Bloody Trail

By the time I located Larkin's Pawnshop, I was still wiping away the tears of mascara that left lines going down my face. Once I had gotten a handle on myself and looked presentable, I walked up to the doorway and read the window sign.

SORRY, WE MISSED YOU.
CLOSED FOR THE DAY.
WILL REOPEN AT 9:00 a.m.

Abruptly I turned and nearly bumped into a lady passing by. I offered my sincere apology, and then I asked her for help. She noticed my red eyes and handed me a tissue. Then she gave me directions to Bakersfield's Holiday Inn.

The Holiday Inn was huge. It was next to the airport which provided everything a traveler would need; restaurant, gift shop, clothing store, and car rentals. I picked a few things out at the clothing store, and then I registered for a "deluxe" room.

The room was spacious, about the same size as some apartments. Except for the windows, which were designed like giant portholes, the type you'd find on an old school ship. The twin bedrooms were very chic, with stylish loud colored ceramic furniture. Each loft was equipped with an extra-large vanity mirror. One room contained a shower and the other a bath. I chose the one with the bath and lounged for almost an hour. Then I called room service and got them to send up a snack. The hop brought me a variety of freshly diced fruit. I chose to eat mostly apple slices with Monterey Jack cheese. Along with that, came a bottle of Chenin Blanc, the complementary house wine.

Before getting dressed, I paraded in the mirror and checked myself out. My tummy was still flat, my hips were firm, and my tits were okay. They were full with no sag. I checked them for lumps. And no cellulite on my thighs, at least not yet, "Hey-hey-hey!" I promised myself that once I got settled in Europe, I'd hire a personal trainer to help get me into shape. I was trying to cheer myself up, but my body and mind was on a spin cycle, as if I were in a giant washing machine. I was on the verge of being sick.

I decided on roughing it. The desert nights are cold, so I chose black skinny-jeans, a white thermal top, black and white Jordan high-tops, a Raiders jacket, and a grey wool beanie. I also carried a black gear bag and my nickel plated Raven .25 caliber automatic, stuffed inside my left hip pocket.

I was anxious. It was only 5:30 p.m. so I gave My Lai a call. "Hmm..." My signal was low but still I got no answer. Maybe she's in a cellphone's dead zone.

* * *

They came right before dusk, through the desert and over the sand dunes. They were camouflaged by the backdrop of a yellowish orange, purple and gray painted sky. Two five-man teams, riding in off-road SUV's. As they moved in, the dust swirled behind each of their Jeep Wrangler Sport's. They knew their target was a decorated military vet, a hand picked member of a Special Forces unit, suited for reconnaissance teams during the Afghan war.

My Lai was waiting for them. There was no hope in catching her by surprise. She took down the first two assassins with a crossbow, another with a silencer, and the fourth with a tactical knife.

The six remaining killers retreated, and so did My Lai. They were forced to regroup and adjust their strategy. However, ten minutes later they rushed the cabin door. Bursting through, they used a stun-gun-type device that worked like a grenade. One of the assassins pulled the pin, then came a blinding light and "Boom!". It was loud as a shotgun blast, enough to wake the dead. Before the smoke cleared, they blasted everything in sight-tables, sofas, chairs, stove, books, blankets and linen with automatic gunfire, bursting from Russian made AK-47's.

The sound of My Lai starting the car — followed by the immediate roar of the engine as she pressed the gas pedal and the four-barrel carburetor opened up — was the last thing the killers heard. Because by that time, it was too late. The digital timer on the hidden explosive device had zeroed out. Suddenly, four Kevlar-body-armored wearing bodies went flying 20 feet into the air, right along with the cabin's roof.

The Camaro's Baja Claw tires were designed to make trails where there were none. They had the toughness to bulldoze their way through the most treacherous terrain. But My Lai couldn't outrun a shoulder-fired rocket launcher, once the coordinates were locked in.

The Camaro's gas tank erupted, jolting, then catapulting the vehicle for at least a hundred yards. From the distance, a red and yellow flash against a turquoise and blue sky emerged, looking like a fiery meteorite had plunged directly into the earth where desert meets twilight.

Slick and Wookie were speeding down Interstate 5, when they noticed the strange & eerie light in the sky. So they rushed over to see what they could. The wreckage from the rocket launcher was gruesome. The rocket's impact, explosion and the burning flames that resulted left My Lai unrecognizable to onlookers. It would take dental records to identify her. Twenty minutes later, Wookie gave Larkin a call.

"Hey, Boss Hog! It's Wookie. Just checkin' in. You need anything?"
"Not tonight. Everything's fine. I'll probably be closing early."
"Ooh, why's that?"

Larkin hesitates for a moment, then whispers... "I got another client in the store who just dumped off a shit load of them stones."

"Is that the same bitch like the last time?"

"Oh-no, this one's a tall redhead, a good-lookin' gal."

"Oh yeah!" Wookie pushed a button on his cellphone, activating the speaker-phone option, then turned the phone's volume up so Slick could listen in. "Did she give you a name?"

"Aaahh, yeah... I'm lookin' over her I.D. right now... Blackwell, a Roxanne Blackwell."

*   *   *

I grabbed my gear and drove back to Larkin's place. I was in luck, as soon as I found a parking space, I saw someone flip the sign after they entered the shop. It read, 'Open from 9:00 til' 9:00'. Once again, I grabbed my gear and zigzagged my way through Main Steet's evening traffic, and slipped through the pawnshop's door.

My sudden appearance must have startled the shopkeeper. He spun around and looked me over with owl eyes.

"How may I help you!" he said in a voice that was louder than necessary.

"Are you, Mr. Larkin?"

"Yes I am."

"Here." I handed him my gear bag and he gave me another odd look, like I'd just insulted him or something.

"What's in it?" he said staring back at me. He didn't touch the bag.

The old man failed to realize that I was in a bit of a hurry, so I unzipped the bag and dumped the diamonds on the counter.

Larkin throws his palms up, "Wait...wait right there!" he uttered with some excitement. He walked to the front door with a little more urgency to his shuffle. He flipped the window sign, dimed the lights and triple locked the door. He returned to me at the counter, reached under it, and brought out bags of miniature green and blue Tupper Ware containers with lids. Each soft plastic tub was no bigger than four-by-four and maybe three inches deep. It took him almost an hour to test and fill them with the majority of my stones. Once he had them all lined up they took up half the counter.

"These twelve tubs are one and one half carat," he said in a raspy voice. "They're carmines, and they carry the most value," he said.

"How much?"

"Dealer's price...ooh, about six to eight mil," he said.

"And the rest?" I ask.

"Two to three million tops."

"Look, I'm in a big hurry, Doc, and you've wasted a lot of my time telling me something I already know. If you're interested in buying the stones, I'll take a half a mil in cash and a five million transfer to my bank in the Bahamas." I hesitated a moment to glance at the pawnshop's clock, it was 7:30 p.m. "But, it's gotta' happen tonight like within the next hour," I said, looking him directly in his owl eyes.

The old man was looking back at me like he had just shot up a nickel bag of heroin, but he wasn't satisfied and he was looking to bang some more. He pulled off his Ben Franklins and squinted. I could tell his eyes were failing him and he needed more light.

"What did you say your name was?"

"I didn't say, but if we're doing business tonight then here's my I.D., and my alias. You'll be needing them to complete the wire transfer."

Larkin offered me his hand. I shook it and gave him my card.

Then he put his glasses on and read the card. "Ms. Blackwell, now I'll tell you what I can do," his owl eyes were beaming. "I can give you two-hundred and fifty thousand in cash and wire three million to your account, tonight."

I said nothing, because there was nothin to say. I looked back at him and smiled. His breathing appeared labored. It really wasn't a good time to have this man tap out on me.

We entered a cluttered back room that looked like Radio Shack or Circuit City. The back room was filled with boxes on top of boxes and a gang of electronic gadgetry. Then his cell phone warbled. He excused himself, and walked away to talk in private. It took almost another forty minutes to do the bank account transfers on computer. Finally, I had to help him move a steel cabinet from where his floor safe was hidden below. He was so excited; he miscounted and gave me three hundred grand. I shoved four stacks of hundreds under each armpit and in my bosom and shoved the remainder in my bag. It was almost 9:00 p.m. when he led me to the back door, but when he opened it, Slick and some other guy were lurking in the alley only a few feet from the exit.

"Hold up, Larkin!" hollered the other guy, "We comin' in!"

They were wearing black three-quarter length trench coats and I wondered why, because it wasn't that cold, nor was it raining outside. Then it dawned on me... Larkin hadn't taken time to close or cover his safe.

"My customer was just leaving, fellas."

"No, she ain't!" meows Slick picking at his front teeth with a white strip of dental floss.

"Hell, woman, I thought you was dead."

He and his friend pushed us back inside and closed the extra thick metal plated burglar proof door. Slick never took his eyes off of me. He was checking me out and salivatin' like a plantation owner preparing to rape another young slave victim.

"Wookie, meet Roxanne," said Slick now grinning. "She's the chick I once told you about... Miss Candy Cane in the flesh. She was a natural, Wookie. Born to eat a dick!" He and Wookie got jokes so they he-hawed it up.

"Fuck ya'll niggas, if you two Gypsy Jokers ain't got somethin' real important to say to me," I glance at Slick 's cheap imitation of a Rolex, "then adios, I'm outta' here, cuz someone's expecting me."

"If it's that robotic lookin' Asian chick you plan on meetin', well, she done gone bye-bye," replied Slick still grinning.

My face paled. My intuition warned me earlier that something had gone awry. It had been a couple hours since I'd heard from My Lai.

"What do you mean?" I ask, not flinching due to the context of his comments.

"We saw the explosion from the freeway," said Wookie. "It lit up the whole sky. We went down to investigate. The whole place had been gutted out and tossed up, like a suicide bomber from the Taliban had been there."

"Well, sorry to hear that, fellas, but I'd like to close up now," said Larkin who was anxious to get everyone out so he could go back to playing with his newly purchased stones. He had no idea what the situation was really all about.

"Hold tight, Old Man!" commanded Slick. "Get her bag, Wookie, cuz she clutchin' it like she got a bomb in it. Let's see what'cha got in there, Miss Candy Cane!" whined Slick like a kid singing a nursery rhyme.

I didn't protest. I tossed my gear bag to Wookie like I was launching a basketball. It thudded against his chest. He quickly unzipped it and dumped out the cash.

"Motha-Fuck!" howled Slick. "You been owing me and it's about time you paid up. Now get the fuck out, Bitch, before I have Wookie bust a cap in yo' freckled-face ass."

"Leave my client alone!" shouted Larkin now holding his Glock 17 and pointing it towards Slick's shoes."

Wookie and Slick look at each other and burst out laughing.

"Who is you?" said Slick still laughing,

"Captain Save a Ho!"

"Wookie! You know where Boss Hog keeps his stash?"

"I sure do!"

"BOOM!" Lightening quick, Slick swung a short handled pump from under his trench and shoots Larkin in the side of his neck. He must of hit an artery because the blood gushed from the old man's body.

Until then, I had never been that close up on death before. Larkin shrieked. Globs of mucus spewed from his mouth. His body was twitching before it hit the floor and there was this foul odor that seemed to get trapped inside my nose and throat.

"You'd best get out of my sight with the quickness, Bitch, befo' I change my mind."

Slick 's blood-shot red eyes made him look like Lucifer himself. I still had my .25 in my hip pocket. I could have easily gotten the drop on Slick, but with Wookie on my right, I might not live to see him die. I bolted out the back door and raced for My Lai's truck.

Was I lucky or was it just fate? I never knew if it was my place to even ask myself that question. I was so frightened by what I had just witnessed, I decided against going back to the hotel. Instead, I pulled up at a Quick Stop and bought two utility flashlights.

I searched through the rubble of My Lai's cabin. It was close to an hour before I quit. Then I searched outside. I found her. Her torso was lying by the ruins of the Camaro's torched out frame. Her body was in parts. I collected them. I must of cried the whole time. I buried her under the almond tree, only twelve feet from where we had our picnic. I'm not a religious person, but I didn't know what else to do. Yeah, I believe in an afterlife, and that we all hopefully end up at a better place, so I tried to pray. It took me a while.

Lord, Please watch over...Me Lie Smith, Sarah Lee, and Lucy Liu. And please take care of... Cathy Wilson, Bones, and Wilma Sarpy too... Amen.

* * *

The caw of crows woke me and the sun blinded my face. The echoes from the distant freeway traffic made the cars seem a lot closer than they really were.

I made a trip to the well and threw water on my face and took a drink. I saw my reflection and for a while I stared. Then I saw Mugsy's face looking back at me and he was barking. I didn't know what to think or what the vision was trying to tell me. Maybe he was just letting me know that he was okay.

My stomach growled. I cranked the engine on My Lai's truck and drove. I ended up at a Quick Stop in the town of Santa Clarita. The parking lot was crowded with migrant workers waiting for some farmer to come by and offer them work. I went inside for coffee and came out stirring my cup. There was a truck parked next to mine, same color with a similar trailer bed attached. People were sitting inside the cab. Before I had a chance to unlock my truck's door, a female voice called out to me.

It was Tracy, a girl I met at Miss Kenny's poolside garden party several months ago. Tracy was actually one of Karrene's college sorority friends. She climbed down from the cab and wobbled over toward me. She was — what looked like to be at least six or eight months pregnant. She was holding her side like it was painful to walk.

"Ooou Roxanne, so nice to see you again," she said smiling then taking a deep breath. With her belly protruding there was no room to hug her, so I walked her over to a bench and helped her sit down.

"How close are you, Tracy?"

"Oooh, I guess about a month, but it feels like any day now. And what about you?"

'I'm-I'm, I'm okay." My coffee was too hot but I drank it any way while I cautiously surveyed people coming and going throughout the parking lot. I knew Tracy was hawk-eyeing me, because I felt her eyes trying to peer inside my brain. Actually, she was staring at my moppy hair and dusty clothes, since the last time she saw me I was shining like new money. Damn it seems like such a long time ago, but I can still remember getting all dolled up, looking fresh and clean in chic designer clothes and having a good time at the pool party in Berkeley with all them sorority chicks. However, this morning I never took time to look at myself in a mirror. There was no telling what kind of mucus might be clinging to my face. So I patted my hair and tried to smooth out the wrinkles in my coat.

"Who's the father?" I aked trying my best to get Tracy's attention off of me.

"That's my husband over there," she said pointing to her truck. "I'm Mrs. Ventura now." She raised her left hand and showed me a diamond ring.

"Congratulations, what a gorgeous ring!" I said trying to manufacture some cheer in my voice. The ring looked expensive. It was huge and sparkled, a cluster of multi-colored jewels. Finally, her husband stepped out of the truck and walked over to where we were seated. His surname was Ventura but most people called him El Topo, which means "The Mole". He was a Mohado, a border brother who had no official papers to live or work in the U.S.

Tracy once had a cocaine habit and El Topo held the clavo, the sack. She became a regular customer and one thing led to another and he ended up getting her pregnant. She said marrying him kept him from getting deported and he never charged her for the drugs because he liked her from the start. Tracy wasn't a whore. She was just a spoiled rich girl who's people had money and lots of it. They cut her off when she married El Topo Ventura, The Mole.

She was five-eleven and her husband was three inches shorter. He had dark hair, a nice build, keen brown eyes, and a hearty smile. Some of his teeth were capped in gold. He wore a tan felt, five gallon cowboy hat, a black sling-shot top, khakis, and snake skin boots. He also wore a jeweled belt that was mostly made of silver. His arms were covered in colorful tattoos

"Quien es esa mujer?" (Who is that, woman?)

"Es mi amiga de Berkeley." (It's my friend from Berkeley)

"Que es que quiere?" (What does she want?)

"Ella quiere crusar la fronteria." (She wants to go with us across the border)

"En Mexico?"

'Si (yes), Ella necesita documentos y una persona para que la guia a su destino." (She needs documents and a person to guide her to her destination)

"Where is that?" said El Topo now speaking in almost perfect English.

"She didn't say," answers Tracy giving me a renewed curious look.

I reached inside my top and pulled out a wad of cash. Both their eyes widened. "I have money to pay," I said to El Topo. "What is your price?"

"There is no price," he replied. "A friend of my wife is my friend as well. We will help you. Do you plan to follow us in your truck?"

His courtesy and candor surprised me. I really hadn't fully figured out my plan yet. All I knew was I needed to get out of the U.S., get the right papers, and get on a plane. I didn't know exactly who I was running from but I knew I couldn't take a chance on continuing to drive My Lai's truck. The two of them were looking at me like I was a crazy person. I guess I looked lost and dazed.

"No," I said, finally answering his question, "if you don't mind, I'll ride with you. But first, I need to get something to eat."

* * *

They took me to a restaurant near a small lake. There had to be a dump site nearby because the stench of sewage was choking everybody out. The name of the place was Siete Mares, it meant "Seven Seas". It was an old wooden building on stilts. The wood's foundation was damp. There were white mini-sea shells on the ground mixed with puddles of water and mud. The porch steps creaked and the door's frame was leaning to one side. I guess it was probably a flood zone and maybe the building had been nearly covered in water at one time.

Once inside, the spot was packed with loud and noisy customers who appeared to be having a good time. I was told that it was always this way because the food was incredibly delicious.

I ordered Ceviehe and Pescado ala diabla, which is a fillet and a catfish. I cleaned my plate and drank two bottles of Corona. I was famished.

The Ventura's had a camper shell. I was tired, so they made room so I could lie in it. I had a fitful sleep. I had dreams of border patrol agents pulling us over and searching our things. I'd wake up and realize we were moving, then I'd fall back to sleep.

I never witnessed the actual border crossing into Mexico. When Tracy woke me up we were parked in the driveway of their home, a village called Rosarito, just south of Tijuana. I rested there for two days. Tracy took me on shopping trips to Tijuana where I bought travel bags and some new clothes. I was paranoid. Everywhere I went I wore designer shades to conceal my identity. When men stared at me too long, I'd scan their bodies looking for anything resembling a dragon tattoo. El Topo wanted to drive me to the city of Chihuahua. He said the arrangements of documents could be done much quicker and easier there. But I didn't want to travel into the interior of Mexico. I'd read too many stories about tourists being abducted and held for ransom. So I took my chances with a Coyote who knew a guy, who knew another guy. Once my papers were in order I made flight reservations for the Bahamas.

It was October 31st, two days before the celebration of "The Day of the Dead". Many people were already wearing skeleton or ghoulish mask. It was the day My Lai was supposed to return Hash Patel's diamonds. She had said the diamonds would lead down a bloody trail, so I wondered what would happen to Slick and Wookie. How long would it be before the long arm of the mob finds them?

I said my goodbyes to the Ventura's and thanked them repeatedly. They gave me their phone number and I promised that once I was settled I'd send them an invite and pay for their flights so they could spend some time in Europe. Still playing it safe, I never told them my exact destination. My first impulse was to arrive in the Bahamas and immediately change my flight plan to Ghana, but the Ebola Virus was still a major threat, and it was now infecting thousands of African people, so I made other plans.

When my flight touched down in the Bahamas, there was a three hour lay-over. I never left the airport lounge. By 3:00 a.m. I was sipping on a rum and coke in the Paradise Hotel. I was told that Jimmy's shift would start at five. It kinda' startled me when he showed up early.

"Hello, Roxanne. You're a bubbly sight for sore eyes." Jimmy had a deep baritone voice like the singer Barry White. His British accent, mixed with his deep voice made the sounds coming out of his mouth a little hard to listen to without thinking, 'Oh, my God!' He had brown friendly eyes sketched on a dark chocolate face. He was also blessed with a beautiful set of pearly white teeth, which made his smile endearing. Jimmy's dreds were so long they looked like extensions. They weren't the thick and natty kind either.

"What brings you back to Atantis?" he continued. "Is it because this is the center of the earth, or were you living amongst the dead?"

"Jimmy, you have a peculiar way of making a person feel welcomed, and what you just said ain't even funny."

"You're a bobby dazzler with a bounce on your shoulders."

"See, there you go again. What'd you just say and speak American, please."

"I said you're a remarkable person and you're smart."

I give him a half smile because I'm not feeling him right now. He's a charmer but he's also a bit of a jerk. "To answer your earlier question, I'm only going to be on the island for a couple days. I'm just here handling some unfinished business."

"Banks?"

"Un-hun," I nod while I sip my drink.

"Where's Cat? She must be around here someplace, is she up in her room?"

Jimmy had a thing for Cathy Wilson, but she never fully trusted him. Yet, he never let it faze him. I guess he felt that with time he could win her over. I took a few moments to scan the faces of the people sitting at other tables and lowered my tone.

"Ahh. Cathy's dead, Jimmy."

Jimmy looks back at me. His perpetual smile became a thin straight line. "Stop your' arsing about!" he warns

"I'm not kidding, Jimmy, it's true."

"Well, what happened to her?"

"It's a long story, and I don't want to get into it now. I'm just here to get our money then I'm leaving as soon as possible. Where's Ray, you seen him?"

I could tell Jimmy wasn't feeling my short and abrupt non-explanation. He left my table to serve another customer without saying a word. Five minutes later he returned with a fresh drink. I guess it was his way of apologizing. Maybe he figured I was still grieving. I lit a cigarette, a 'fag' as Jimmy would say, and we stared at each other in silence for what seemed like quite a while.

"How's Ray?" I reminded him after flicking some ashes and exhaling some smoke.

"You just missed him. He and his wife flew back to the States like a rat out of a drain-pipe, day before yesterday."

"Oh, was there a problem, had something gone wrong?"

"I don't know. Just like you, they didn't share their reasons for being in such a hurry. The banks are under scrutiny in case you didn't know."

"Scrutiny?"

"Yeah, that's what I said, scrutiny. In 2008 the Swiss banks bailed out UBS, a huge international bank, and in 2009 UBS pressured by the U.S. tax authorities agreed to close some twenty thousand hidden offshore accounts. So the banks in Cayman, Virgin Islands, and here ended up disclosing data on about five thousand U.S. citizens. So, once a year the authorities make a random sweep on the islands' old and new accounts."

"Are you sure about this, Jimmy, or are you just speculating on something you think is true?"

"It's not rubbish I say, and it's the wrong time for you to have cloth-ears, Roxanne. But if you're planning on clearing out your accounts, do it first thing in the morning. Then, do a runner."

I finished my drink. Jimmy wanted to give me a re-fill but I refused. I told him I had to get in a few 'winks', what he calls sleep, before I hit the streets. I went back to my room but there was no way I could sleep.

ROXXY

It was already 5:00 a.m. Friday. I began praying that my money was still mine, and that my luck had not run out.

CHAPTER FIFTEEN

Hans Kohl

At 3:00 p.m. Eastern Standard Time, I was boarding Virgin Air, destination Lisbon, Portugal. From there I boarded another plane and was flown to Geneva, Switzerland. Once we were flying over the Atlantic, I felt a sense of relief. I no longer needed to study faces and look at people like I was a cross-eyed fool.

Crossing into Europe's airspace, and checking out the scenery below seemed to put my mind at ease. The landscape and buildings were different, colorful and strange, all at the same time. It was like looking through a kaleidoscope. My mind suddenly became flooded with curious and adventurous thoughts, but my precautious side reminded me to keep my expectations sensible and my emotions in check. I wanted to believe I was leaving all my troubles behind and it seemed that way for a while. I hadn't known it yet, but eventually I would pick up new ones. With a fresh start, I could try to bury the foul memories and let myself forget.

* * *

I had some choices, too many perhaps. I started out in Geneva and I later moved to Lausanne. I liked living near the Geneva Lake because it resembled an ocean beach. Besides, the area was sunnier than the other parts of Switzerland and I wasn't into being cold. It took me awhile to get use to the fog; a thick layer would often hang out for several days.

The people were friendly but mostly out of curiosity, because I couldn't speak any of the most commonly used languages: German, Italian, and French. And the only newspaper in English was The Guardian and it was published by the Brits. Right away I figured out European men thought they were sophisticated and smart. Some approached me with suspicion and others were cheerful and suave. They assumed I was some type of actress from the U.S. In most instances I played right along with it. Then there were the low-budget Sugar Daddies who claimed they wanted to look out for me. Just about every man past middle age acted as if they had royal ties and many introduced themselves as land barons. Maybe there was some truth to it, but I just wasn't interested. I was trying to keep an open mind and retain my sense of humor about things but it was hard because all the people who kept me laughing were dead. I had no real support system except me, myself, and I. At least I wasn't having any bad dreams any more, no suicides or near deaths, although I still sleep with a gun under my pillow.

Then one day, a neighbor offered me a pet that was only two months old. It was a Doberman, red, gangly, and clumsy. It was perfect. I named her Maxine but I called her Max for short.

I hired Hans Kohl, a German cross-trainer who came with good referrals. He was six-two, blond, steel blue eyes, a jawbone like Dudley Do Right's and forearms like Popeye. His resume said he was thirty-six but he looked much older. He reminded me of a macho kind of guy, probably sexually promiscuous and capable of inflicting pain. I didn't hire him for that though, and he turned out to be a well-mannered, quiet, and peaceful sort of guy. He was a sportsman. Most everyone in that area were energetic and fit. Hiking, skiing, bobsledding, and target shooting was a way of life. I wasn't really into the snow scene. I was only there on temporary basis because of my accounts at the banks. But I hired Hans to get me back in shape and we did it with running, swimming, and target shooting, because those sports I enjoyed and they were more my style.

Six months later, I leased a French chateau in Villars les Dombes, The Village of Lakes. The weather was so much nicer in France and it wasn't very far from the Swiss banks. Besides, the money was similar, both countries were dealing in francs. The chateau's layout was closer to a Tudor styled home on twenty-five acre tract, including a small winery. The six rooms and the spacious loft hadn't been occupied for several years. The caretaker had no clue as to why, other than the owners lived in the United States. I hired a few locals to help me spruce it up. I found an older married couple to do the gardening and eventually I entrusted them with housecleaning and being my personal chefs.

When I wasn't outdoors, me and Max spent a lot of time in my loft. It became my nest for books, wardrobe, and a vast collection music and DVD's. It was there I had an ornate rosewood canopied bed built. I had an ornate mirror design mounted on the headboard and another mirror inlaid into the canopy overhead. The room was complemented with a surround sound entertainment system.

Once I got to know him better, I found Hans to be good natured and very attentive to detail. At first he seemed a little aloof like he had a lot on his mind. As time passed, he volunteered to do things for me around the house. Man things, like chop firewood or do mechanical work on my car. I bought a vintage second hand Mercedes Benz, a 1990 classic, grey with silver trimmings. Everything was original except for the motor.

It was in the middle of fall season when Hans asked for a little time off. He said he needed to return to his home, Offenbach, a smaller city just outside of Frankfurt, Germany. He said his father was ill, but he expected not to be gone for no more than a week. Hans was a man of his word, He returned promptly, but I noticed something about his demeanor which was quite different. There was excitement in his steely blue eyes and the once reserved man was oozing with conversation. He came by on a Sunday and caught me completely by surprise. I had given the help the day off and I'd just finished taking my bath. I greeted him wearing a towel turban on my head and the rest of me was wrapped in this peach colored terrycloth robe. I'm quite sure Hans was aroused by my appearance because the sudden lump in his trousers I'm certain was not a gun.

I wasn't ready to do him.

I had abstained from sex for close to a year. I don't know the reason why, but since leaving the States my body seemed to be in shock. Things just felt different in Europe and there was no need to use my body to make money anymore, and I wasn't looking for love. Max was my love and a very jealous protector she was. Although it was kind of peculiar, because she often growled only when Hans was around.

Hans excused himself and went outside to get some firewood. I had managed to get through my first European winter when I arrived in Switzerland but this would be my first winter in France. I had moved here due to the warmer climate, but if the winter was too cold for my blood, I'd be moving further south.

Hans returned with a half cord of wood. He was wearing brown climbing boots and tan cargo shorts. The man obviously had a lot of strength in his arms but he also had big calves and powerful legs. Once he got the fire going, I had a hot mug of Swiss cocoa waiting for him. He drank, and watched me put nail polish on my toes.

While he was visiting his family in Germany, he'd recorded this singing group that was on tour there. He had an MP3 and he wanted me to listen, so I plugged it into my stereo system. Right away, I recognized the old school Jamaican group, they were "The Rubicons", good music to relax by but even better if you're with someone you love.

[Music] ALL OF MY LIFE I'VE DREAMED OF YOU...(dreamed of you)

YOU'RE LIKE A DREAM THATS COMING TRUE
(coming true)

SO MANY TIMES I THOUGHT THAT YOU WERE REALLY MINE...WHY CANT YOU SEE THAT ALL MY LOVE IS PART OF THEE...CAUSE I LOVE   YOU...

(I'm really in love with you)

WHY WOULD I LEAVE YOU...

(I'm really in love with you)
IF I LOVE YOU
WHY WOULD I HURT YOU...

Hans watched me carefully decorate my toes with glitter, then more polish. He was staring and it kind of turned me on. Curious, I handed him the bottle and said I needed help. For a man with thick fingers and chapped dry hands, he had a delicate touch. My eyes traveled to his barrel chest. I'd never seen him without a shirt.

Being the tease that I am I parted my legs ever so slightly. Hans froze and I watched his vision glide slowly up my leg and rest between my thighs. He had a frozen look on his face, not really excitement, tight jawed and silent. He had the look of a little boy who wanted to speak but didn't know what to say.

Then Max wandered over next to me, looked at Hans and yielded a low growl. Hans stopped what he was doing and dug deep into his cargo pocket and pulled out two milk bones. He let Max see it then tossed them over on the fireplace rug. Max let the bones bounce then stop. He looked at me then again at Hans, then off he went. He stretched out in front of the fireplace and munched on the treats.

Hans' next move caught me completely by surprise. He leaned over and scooped my long body into his arms.

"Hans, what do you think you're doing!" I giggled. "Put me down!" I giggled more. I wasn't serious nor was I trying to resist.

Hans grinned. His big arms held me tight and I felt secure. He carried me up the staircase and I peeked around his shoulder and saw that Max had dropped his bone and followed. Hans layed me on my bed and dug into his cargo pocket and came up with another milk bone.

Max had seated himself at the foot of my bed and Hans tried the trick again. He tossed the bone outside the loft's doorway but Max didn't budge.

I laid on my stomach watching their reflection from my headboard mirror, then pivoting on my belly, I used my finger and pointed it towards the door, "Max! Out!" I said in a stern voice.

Max whimpered and hesitantly followed my command and Hans shut the door. I looked back at Hans as though he were a Prussian Prince. He climbed into my bed, straddled my legs, and hiked up my robe. I felt his muscular hands massaging my buttocks. "Hmmm..," I moaned. I turned my face into my pillows. Then I raised my head and peeked back at him. The Rubicons mellow lyrics flooded the loft...

[Music] MAYBE I FAILED TO MAKE YOU UNDERSTAND...(understand) HOW MUCH YOU MEAN TO ME YOU'RE PART OF EVERY PLAN...(every plan)

IN EVERYWAY YOU GET ME THROUGH THE DAY...WHY CAN'T I MAKE YOU SEE THAT YOU'RE MY LOVE YOU'RE PART OF ME...

With my help, Hans removed my robe and began massaging my back, neck, and shoulders. He paused and I felt his tool lodged between my legs. I didn't see him take off his pants, but it didn't matter. The feeling was nice and firm, and him just rubbing up against my pussy caused it to cream.

I looked at his reflection from my headboard mirror and I seen ecstasy on his face. His eyes were closed and his lips were parted. I did not want him to cum too soon so I reach around my back and grabbed him. As I said before, I like a man with a little texture on his dick and Hans had plenty. I rose up and looked at him through the mirror once again. His dick was pretty, a bulbous egg shaped head that looked like a smooth porcelain kitchen tool. It was quite sensual. The color of its skin was a yellowed tan, at least eight inches long, skinny and gnarly in the middle and much thicker and wider near the base. I searched, but I couldn't find his balls.

He moaned. I continued to massage him as though I were strumming an exotic instrument. He seemed to be engrossed in the music. The lead singer sweetly crooned, his voice harmonizing with drums, piano, and French horns.

[Music] CAUSE I LOVE YOU...

(I'm really in love with you)

WHY WOULD I LEAVE YOU...

Hans' skin was very dry. I didn't know if the creamy walls of my uterus would suffice, so I snatched a bottle of body oil from a bedside table and managed to squirt my palm, then applied it to his shaft. He moaned again and I squeezed. It felt so nice just holding it. I didn't want to let go. He hadn't entered me and my sexual frenzy was already on the brink of climax.

My body began to shiver...l tried to hold back. When suddenly...

"Oooooh! Ooooh...aaah."

Hans thrust himself inside me. It took me awhile to catch my breath. He lay there inside me throbbing. The thick cord-like veins of his shaft wouldn't remain still. It felt like he was up in my belly. His dick had stretched to an enormous size.

Hans hadn't climaxed but I did.

The orgasms and shivering wouldn't stop...and for a moment...I think I blacked out.

* * *

[Music] IF I LOVE YOU...
(I'm really in love with you)
WHY WOULD I LEAVE YOU...
(that's because I'm in love with you)
IF I LOVE YOU...
(I'm really in love with you)
WHY WOULD I HURT YOU...

When I awakened, the first thing I heard was the music. Then I heard something rip and tare. I looked into the mirror and Hans had removed his thermal top. He slung it playfully around my neck and began punishing my womb with his swollen yellow dick. The mirror showed that his eyes were open. His steely blues looked icy and wild. The music seemed to get louder, like someone had hit a restart and turned up the volume button. The same tract was playing over again...

...MAYBE I FAILED TO MAKE YOU UNDERSTAND...HOW MUCH YOU MEAN TO ME YOU'RE PART OF EVERY PLAN...

The music began to sound like noise. The melodic voice, the horns and drums suddenly felt eerie. The cheery echo turned into a haunting chant.

Hans seemed to be in some kind of manic trance. Like a robotic machine, he was getting pleasure by digging me out.

Over the music I could hear Max barking. I could hear him scratching the door.

THEN I SAW IT!

Something scrawled on Hans' chest.

The mirror was foggy from our deep breathing and the heat from our body's sweat. The muscles in my throat constricted, so I craned my neck...

I had no voice to shriek.

Hans' fierce eyes were boring into mine.

I couldn't hide my panic.

The veins in his neck were ridged. His shirt was tightly wound around my throat.

His forearms bulged as he twisted it like a tourniquet.

My head was pulled up toward the canopy's overhead mirror. I looked at his chest and I saw...THE DRAGON TATOO!!!!!

Hans was doing what he was sent to do...

KILL ME!!!

[Music] IF I LOVE YOU...

WHY WOULD I LEAVE YOU...

IF I LOVE YOU...

WHY WOULD I HURT YOU!!!

All the faces of my friends who had died flashed across my mind. I didn't hear the music any more. I didn't hear Max scratching or barking at the door either.

I was weak...My body was hot, My energy was drained. My pulse was faint. I was fading...

Then, from somewhere deep in my bowels I mustered a rush of adrenaline.

Suddenly, I could hear the music again...

...IF I LOVE YOU...

...I'M REALLY IN LOVE WITH YOU...

...WHY WOULD I LEAVE YOU...

I willed my fingers to stretch, reaching desperately under the pillow and finally, I got my hand on the gun. THE GLOCK 17 — I always kept near me while I slept.

Hoping to shatter the mirror inlaid into the canopy overhead, I aimed upward and emptied the sixteen round clip.

The glass EXPLODED! It came CRASHING DOWN LIKE THUNDER!!!

I could hear HANS' SCREAMS, as the dagger-like chunks of glass punctured his body!!! Thankfully, he was on top of me and bore the brunt of the large pieces falling on us, because we were both buried beneath an avalance of huge amounts of broken glass.

Hans' body was motionless, and his weight began to get heavier. My arms and head were oozing blood. Somehow, I managed to crawl out from under him and took a good look at the scene.

Hans' back and buttocks was a bloody mess. The shattered glass covering the bed and the floor looked like the diamonds we had stolen, and sold. The same one's that left the bloody trail.

"The Rubicons" lead singer crooned as the French horns swooned...

CAN'T YOU SEE I'M IN LOVE WITH YOU!!!

WHY WOULD I KILL YOU!!

This ending might have turned out better for me and my crew if My Lai hadn't been so caught up in self-interest and revenge. The real truth is we were all greedy and thinking of ourselves. I was supposed to be the stable-one, the sharp-one who made all the right moves. But this time 'The Force' wasn't my ally and them' damn diamonds and deaths of my friends is why I'm buried in sorrow and so much pain. But like my momma once told me...

"Child, God don't like ugly, and one day he gon' let you reap whatever you done sowed!" I knew I came a long way... And by the grace of God...I am thankful that I'll live to fight another day.

THE END

About the Author

Alec 'Alex Briggs' Bellard hails from the heart of Silicon Valley, San Jose, California; a former electronics drafting designer and technical school instructor. Bellard began with children's stories and progressed into adult short fiction and novels. Bellard is the winner of Oakland Bay Area Writers of Color and Distinct Award (2007) and was awarded New York's Dawson Prize (2010).

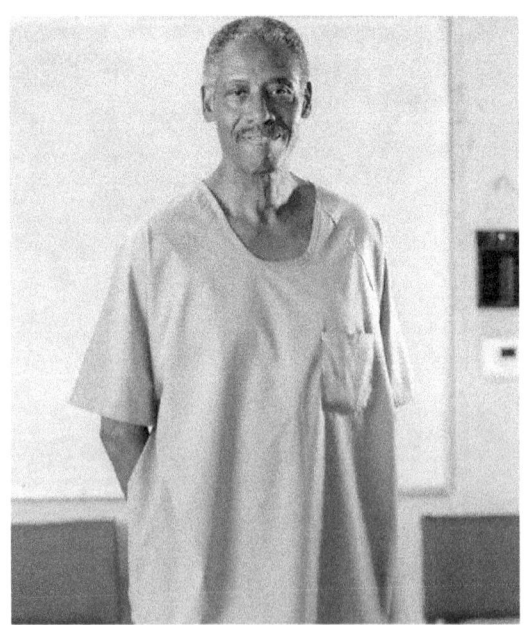

A.C. BELLARD
AKA
ALEX BRIGGS

Capital Gaines LLC presents "ROXXY", an exotic suburban thriller!

A.C. Bellard, aka Alex Briggs is an award winning author out of Silicon Valley.

He won Won 'New York's PEN American Centers Dawson Prize in 2010 for "Walk like a man, a childhood memoir, and he's published a hit serial novel, : Bonesteel: Cold As Ice."

He is presently working on "Roxxy II"

Alex gives special acknowledgments to Spanish language contributors: Candelario, "Pantera" and R. Ventura, "Toons".

Roxxy is dedicated to Alex's daughter, Tabora K. Briggs, granddaughter, Natale, and grandson, Kimani Freeman,

Love, Peace, & Prosperity,

Alex

aka A.C. Bellard

Available Now...

@www.amazon.com

It's Hard Being The Same. By Eric Curtis

Roxxy. By A.C. Bellard

Ideas More Powerful Than Force. By Ricky Gaines II

Neologic Thought. By Ah'Khemu

Coming Soon...

Street Karma by Leo Fountila IV

Only A Chosen Few by Mack Malik

✻ ✻

For ordering info please visit our website or call
www.capgainesllc.com –302-433-6777

CAPITAL GAINES LLC
4023 Kennett Pike #2082
Wilmington, Delaware 19807
www.capgainesllc.com
Telephone: (415-857-5433)
Email: cg@capgainesllc.com

MAIL PAYMENT TO:

CAPITAL GAINES LLC
4023 Kennett Pike #2082   ORDER YOUR BOOKS AND HAVE THEM DELIVERED QUICKLY
Wilmington, Delaware 19807

TITLE OF BOOK	QUANTITY EACH	TOTAL QUANTITY	METHOD OF PAYMENT	PRICE EACH	TOTAL PRICE
IDEAS MORE POWERFUL THAN FORCE				$15.00	
IT'S HARD BEING THE SAME				$15.00	
ROXXY				$15.00	
TRIUMPH				$10.00	
NEOLOGIC THOUGHT				$10.00	
STREET KARMA				$15.00	
ONLY A CHOOSEN FEW				$15.00	
TOTAL					

FROM:	SHIP TO:
NAME: ADDRESS: CITY/STATE/ZIP CODE: PHONE: EMAIL:	NAME: ADDRESS: CITY/STATE/ZIP CODE: